**JAMES PATTERSON** is one of the best-known and biggest-selling writers of all time. His books have sold in excess of 300 million copies worldwide and he has been the most borrowed author in UK libraries for the past nine years in a row. He is the author of some of the most popular series of the past two decades – the Alex Cross, Women's Murder Club, Detective Michael Bennett and Private novels – and he has written many other number one bestsellers including romance novels and stand-alone thrillers.

James is passionate about encouraging children to read. Inspired by his own son who was a reluctant reader, he also writes a range of books for young readers including the Middle School, I Funny, Treasure Hunters, House of Robots, Confessions and Maximum Ride series. James is the proud sponsor of the World Book Day Award and has donated millions in grants to independent bookshops. He lives in Florida with his wife and son.

# BOOK**SHOTS**

## STORIES AT THE SPEED OF LIFE

What you are holding in your hands right now is no ordinary book, it's a BookShot.

BookShots are page-turning stories by James Patterson and other writers that can be read in one sitting.

Each and every one is fast-paced, 100% story-driven; a shot of pure entertainment guaranteed to satisfy.

Available as new, compact paperbacks, ebooks and audio, everywhere books are sold.

**BookShots – the ultimate form of storytelling. From the ultimate storyteller.**

# HEIST

## JAMES
## PATTERSON

### WITH *REES JONES*

BOOK**SHOTS**

1 3 5 7 9 10 8 6 4 2

BookShots
20 Vauxhall Bridge Road
London SW1V 2SA

BookShots is part of the Penguin Random House
group of companies whose addresses can be found at
global.penguinrandomhouse.com

First published by BookShots in 2016

www.penguin.co.uk

A CIP catalogue record for this book is available
from the British Library.

ISBN 9781786530110

Typeset in Garamond Premier Pro font 11/15.5 pt in
India by Thomson Digital Pvt Ltd, Noida, Delhi

Printed and bound in Great Britain by Clays Ltd, St Ives Plc

Penguin Random House is committed to a sustainable future
for our business, our readers and our planet. This book is made
from Forest Stewardship Council® certified paper.

# HEIST

# CHAPTER 1

**THE THIEF'S GLOVED FINGERS** beat against the steering wheel, a rhythm as hectic as the young man's darting eyes.

'You're doing it again,' the woman beside him accused, rubbing at her face to drive home her irritation.

The thief turned in his seat, his wild eyes quickly shifting to an angry focus.

She wouldn't meet the stare, he knew. She never did, despite the fact that she was five years his senior, and tried to order him about as if she had the rank and privilege of family.

'Doing what?' He smiled, his handsome face made ugly by resentment.

The woman didn't answer. Instead, she rubbed again at her tired eyes. Her name was Charlotte Taylor, and anticipation had robbed her of any sleep the previous night. Instead she had lain awake, thinking of this day. Thinking of how failure would condemn the man she loved.

Charlotte tried again to hold the gaze of the man beside her, but she couldn't meet his eyes – she saw the past in them.

And what did he see when he looked at her? That a once pretty girl was now cracked from stress and sorrow? That her shoulders stooped like a woman of sixty, not thirty? Charlotte did not want to feel that scrutiny. That obnoxious charity she had suffered from family and strangers for nine years.

'It's OK if you're scared,' she baited the thief, knowing that aggression would be one way to distract her from her niggling thoughts.

'Me? I'm excited,' the younger man shot back.

And he was.

Today was the day. Today was the day when years of talking, months of planning and weeks of practice would pay off.

Lives were going to change, and it would all start here.

'I'm excited,' the thief said again, but this time with a smile.

His name was Alex Scowcroft, an unemployed twenty-five-year-old from north-west England's impoverished coast. Today the thief was far from home, his white panelled rental van parked up beneath a blue October sky on Hatton Garden, the street that was the heart of London's diamond trade.

Charlotte was not excited. In truth, she was sick to her stomach. She had never broken the law – not in any meaningful way, anyway – and the thought of being caught and convicted turned her guts into knots. And yet, the thought of failure was infinitely worse.

As she always did when she needed comfort, Charlotte pulled a blue envelope from the inside pocket of her worn leather jacket. The letter was grimy from oily fingers, and teardrops had smudged the ink. The blue paper was the mark of military correspondence, given to soldiers at war so they could write to their loved ones.

Hoping to take strength from the words, Charlotte looked over the faded letter.

Catching sight of the 'bluey', Scowcroft stopped his fidgeting. 'Was that –'

'His last one.'

'He never wrote me any letters.' Scowcroft smiled. 'Knew I couldn't write one back.'

Charlotte folded the letter away, replacing it into the pocket that would keep it closest to her heart.

'You're his brother, Alex. You two don't need to put words on paper to know how you feel about each other.'

Uncomfortable at the sincerity in her words, Scowcroft could only manage a violent nod before turning his gaze back out of the window, his chest sagging with relief as he saw a man approaching.

'Baz is back.'

Gaunt-faced and stick thin, Matthew Barrett entered the van through its sliding door and pushed his bony skull into the space between Charlotte and Scowcroft.

'Same as it's been every day,' he told them in a voice made harsh by smoking only the cheapest cigarettes. 'The shops are opening. No sign of any extra security. If he sticks to the same pattern again today, our man should be here in ten.'

Scowcroft exhaled hard with anticipation. 'Get your gear on.'

Behind him, Barrett changed from the street clothes of his reconnaissance into a similar style of assault boot and biker jacket worn by his two accomplices. Finally, he pulled a baseball cap tight onto his head, and brought up the thin black mask that would obscure his features. Eyeing himself in the mirror, Barrett thought aloud: 'Assume that we've been spotted as soon as we pull off. Don't try to be stealthy. Maximum violence. We get out. We shock. We grab. We extract.'

'I know the plan,' Scowcroft grunted.

'I know you do, mate,' Barrett told him with the patience of a mentor. 'But there's no such thing as going over it too many times. Five minutes,' he concluded, looking at the van's dashboard clock.

Scowcroft turned the ignition, and four minutes passed with nothing but the throb of the van's diesel engine for distraction. It was Charlotte who broke the silence.

'If they get me, but you two pull this off, I don't want Tony to see me in prison. I don't want him to see me like that.'

Barrett reached out and placed a gloved hand on her shoulder. 'Since when does anyone tell Tony what to do? He loves you, Char, and when he's back to us, he'd be seeing you on Mars if that's what it took.'

Charlotte eased at the words and rolled down her balaclava, her piercing blue eyes afire with righteous determination.

'For Tony, then.'

'For Tony,' the two men echoed, voices thick with grit and love.

Barrett looked again at the van's dashboard. 'Five minutes is up.'

In the driver's seat, Scowcroft's fingers began to beat against the steering wheel once more.

'He's here,' he told them, and put the van into gear, pulling out into the lazy traffic of a Friday mid-morning.

A few pedestrians, mostly window-shoppers, ambled along the pavements, but Scowcroft's eyes were focused solely on a burly skinhead who looked as if he'd been plucked from a prison cell and clad in Armani. More precisely, Scowcroft focused on what was in the man's hand – a leather holdall. A leather holdall that would change their lives.

The big man's stride was slow and deliberate. Scowcroft reduced the van's speed to a running pace and glided close to the kerb.

The moment had come.

'Go!' he shouted, overcome by excitement.

Then, as they had practised dozens of times, Charlotte threw open the heavy passenger door so that the metal slammed into the big man's back, the leather holdall flying free as he collapsed onto the pavement.

'He's dropped it, Baz! Go!' Scowcroft shouted again as he stood on the brakes. Barrett threw himself from the van's sliding door, his eyes scanning for the bag and finding it beneath a parked car.

'I see it!' Barrett announced from outside, but Scowcroft's eyes were elsewhere. And widening in alarm.

'Shit,' he cursed.

He'd expected to see pedestrians flee the scene. He'd expected to see a brave one try to interfere. But what Scowcroft had not expected to see was two motorcycles coming at them along the pavement, the riders hidden ominously behind black visors.

With gut instinct, Scowcroft knew that the bikers were coming for the contents of the bag.

'Shit!' he repeated, then spat, because years of talking, months of planning and weeks of practice were about to come undone.

So Alex Scowcroft formulated a new plan. One which any Scowcroft would have made.

He reached beneath his seat and pulled his older brother's commando dagger from its sheath. Charlotte saw the blade the moment before she saw the incoming bikers, and grasped the implications. She looked to Scowcroft for leadership.

'Would you die for my brother?' he asked her.

She nodded, swallowing the fear in her throat.

'Would you kill for him?'

Her eyes told him that she would.

'Then get out and fight.'

# CHAPTER 2

**SCOWCROFT AND CHARLOTTE FLEW** from the van's doors like fury, adrenaline coursing through their veins.

'Baz!' Scowcroft shouted. 'Leave the bag where it is and get over here! We've got a problem!'

'Leave the bag?' Charlotte questioned aghast, a ball hammer in her shaking hands.

'They'll snatch it and go. We need them off those bikes.'

With no sign of the holdall, the black-helmeted riders slowed their pace. Scowcroft could feel their gaze now falling on him and his two accomplices from behind the tinted visors.

Barrett came running up beside the others.

'The bag's by the front-left wheel arch. I can grab it quick, but what about them?' he asked, then took in the sight of Scowcroft's commando dagger. For a moment, Scowcroft thought Barrett would tell him to put the weapon away. Instead, Barrett drew an identical blade from a sheath on his lower leg.

'Just remember, drive the blade, don't slice,' Barrett encouraged the younger man, brandishing his own dagger in an attempt to scare off the riders and avoid bloodshed.

It didn't work.

The bikers had their own weapons – five hundred pounds of metal, and that metal could reach sixty miles per hour in the time it took to close the gap to Scowcroft and his companions.

The bikes revved hard, leaving rubber on the pavement. Side by side, they came forward in a cavalry charge of steel.

Barrett and Charlotte darted left and pressed themselves into the cover of a shallow doorway, but Scowcroft dived for the hold-all beneath the wheel arch, the bikers aiming for the easy target of his exposed body. They saw the chance to cripple the man as he grasped for his prize, and engines roared louder as throttles were held open.

Then, as his accomplices waited for the dreadful moment of impact, Scowcroft pressed his body down into the tarmac, squeezing himself beneath the car, and flung the holdall into the face of the closest rider.

The bikers had taken the bait, and now they paid the price. Travelling at sixty miles per hour, the rider was hit by the light leather bag as if by a baseball bat, whipping his neck and sending both bike and rider skidding across the pavement. With great skill, the fallen rider's partner was able to avoid entanglement, but it brought him to a stop.

'On him!' Scowcroft shouted, rushing to collect the bag.

Charlotte and Barrett broke from the refuge of the doorway and sprinted towards the second biker. The rider tried to twist on his seat, reaching down for a blade concealed in his boot, but Barrett was quicker and hit the rider with a rugby tackle, his own dagger flying free in the collision. The two men and the bike crashed to the floor, Barrett crying out in pain as his leg became pinned beneath the hot metal of the engine, and grunting in agony again as the rider headbutted him with his helmet. As the pouring blood soaked his balaclava, Barrett was forced to remove his mask.

'Charlotte!' he gasped. 'My dagger!'

Charlotte looked around desperately for the blade, but when she saw where it was, the discovery caused her to go rigid with panic.

The blade was in the hand of the bag's courier. Recovered from the initial ambush, the big man was on his knees, aggressively turning the van's tyres into husks of useless rubber.

Without thinking of her own safety, Charlotte charged towards him, but Scowcroft beat her to it and drove his blade into the man's shoulder. The big man roared in agony and tried to turn his captured dagger towards Scowcroft, but the wound had severed muscle and the arm hung limp and useless by his side. Scowcroft kicked the blade from the man's hand and followed by planting his steel toecap into the man's jaw. Barely conscious, the burly man slumped backwards against the van, leaving a smear of blood against the white panelling.

Pinned beneath the bike, Barrett and the rider continued their own struggle, the helmet crashing again into Barrett's broken nose.

Scowcroft and Charlotte arrived to haul the bike off the pair. Then Barrett pulled himself clear as Charlotte threw herself at the rider, her furious punches wasted against the protection of his helmet and thick jacket.

'Get off him!' Scowcroft called out. Barrett gritted his teeth and dragged Charlotte back by her shoulders, leaving Scowcroft free to push the bike back on top of the sprawling rider.

'I've got the bag,' he panted. 'But the van's done.'

Barrett looked over his shoulder, blood bubbling from his shattered nose. A few curious heads were poking out of windows, but most of Hatton Garden's diamond traders had bolted their doors at the first sign of trouble.

'Get the backpacks out the van,' Scowcroft told them. 'Come on, let's go!'

'There's no sirens,' Barrett observed as Charlotte handed out the small backpacks, each one unique in design and colour. 'Where the hell are the coppers?'

'Who cares?' Scowcroft countered. 'We got what we came for. Let's get out of here!'

Without waiting for agreement, Scowcroft made for the nearest alleyway. Charlotte and Barrett followed in his wake, leaving three groaning bodies on the pavement.

Not one of them saw the pinstripe-suited gentleman in the window of Swiss Excellence, a specialist diamond jeweller. If they had, perhaps they would have noticed that the man's manicured hand was shaking as it picked up a telephone from its cradle. Perhaps they would have assumed that the pinstripe-suited gentleman was finally calling the police.

They'd have been wrong.

'Hello, sir,' the jeweller began, with deference born of fear. 'I'm afraid . . .' He swallowed. 'I'm afraid that someone has stolen your diamonds.'

The line clicked dead.

# CHAPTER 3

**DETECTIVE INSPECTOR ANDREW HILL** was sitting behind his desk in Scotland Yard.

'Well, technically I'm FaceTiming you from the office,' he told his wife of three weeks. 'It's bloody purgatory, Deb. I've got no cases. All my paperwork is done. I'm like the ghost of a young girl who was murdered in a Victorian manor. My soul can't find peace, and all I have to look forward to is jumping out on you when you use the bathroom.'

'I told you I'd stab you if you do that again.' Deb laughed on the phone's screen. 'Now stop being a melodramatic arse and find something to do. Get working on the business.'

'I'm not allowed to work a second job until I get the redundancy,' Hill grumbled.

'Yes you are.'

'Well, OK, yeah, but it's frowned upon. I don't want to rub anyone up the wrong way before I leave. You never know who's going to be useful for business,' the detective protested through a smile.

'I'm just hearing a lot of gas. Anyway, some of us do have to work. I'll see you tonight, babe. Love you.'

'Love you too.'

His call ended, Hill checked his emails and texts for the tenth time that hour. Entering his podcast app, he scrolled through a dozen shows on entrepreneurship and business management. Hitting refresh, Hill searched in vain for a new episode.

'Bloody purgatory,' he groaned under his breath. He reached for his briefcase and opened it, pulling a sheaf of bound papers from within.

These were Hill's business plans, drawn up over the past two years, and he spent the next hour poring over them, even though every detail was ingrained in his memory. As a regular gym-goer, and former centre for the national police rugby team, Hill had been looking for a way to turn his passion for fitness into a career. Two years ago, he'd finally found it.

Hill wanted to create a national chain of gyms, but he also knew that 80 per cent of independent gyms failed in their first five years of business. Hill didn't intend to become one of those failures. Instead, he would buy those that did fold, streamline them, and so grow his own chain of twenty-four-hour, low-cost fitness centres.

All he needed was money.

He had scrimped and saved what he could, but living in central London sapped even a detective inspector's fifty thousand a year. Deb had insisted on the finest ring and wedding, and soon she'd want a family. Both in their mid-thirties, that day would have to come sooner rather than later, and with it the bills. Always the bloody bills.

So Hill had snatched at the opportunity for voluntary redundancy that the police budget cuts had mandated, and the package would almost give him enough money to buy the first of the failing gyms. It was a small step in what he saw as the beginning of an empire. Having studied the markets and gone over the figures until he saw them in his sleep, Hill was now desperate for the day of his redundancy and the beginning of his new life.

Until then he was bored. Frustrated and bored. So he went in search of something to occupy him.

He found it in the form of Detective Inspector David Morgan. The Welshman was a drinking partner of Hill's after a long day or a trying case.

'You look like someone pissed in your tea, Mo,' Hill greeted his friend. 'What's up?'

Morgan was pulling his winter coat over his thick shoulders.

'Got a right stinker of a job, mate. Just about to call it a day for the weekend, and they shaft me with a bloody robbery in Hatton Garden.' Morgan sniffed, gesturing at the notes on his desk.

'Diamonds?' Hill asked with interest.

'Take a look.'

Hill picked up the notes, flicking quickly through.

'So this wasn't called in by a jeweller's, and none of them have reported anything stolen?' Hill assessed, eyes narrowing.

'That's right. The robbery was a snatch and grab on the street. Except it was more like a Royal bloody Rumble than a snatch and grab, by the sounds of it. The witness's details are in there.'

'Who the hell does a street robbery in Hatton Garden?' Hill posed, puzzled. The high-end area was awash with CCTV. 'And the uniforms didn't get there until everyone had vanished?'

'Exactly. Hence why I'll be in all bloody weekend. This one's got organised crime written all over it. It should be the NCA's case, but they won't touch it unless there's something tangible. So it looks like I won't get to watch Wales smash the French.'

'You go, mate. I'll take the job,' Hill said, shocking the Welshman.

'Bollocks, man, it's your last week.'

'It'll be my last week on the planet if I don't find something to keep me busy. And this has got something to it, I can tell.'

Morgan was unconvinced, so Hill came clean.

'You know what the last case I closed was, don't you?' he asked his friend.

Morgan knew. Everyone knew. It was one of those stories that circulated around the station like wildfire.

A young woman had been murdered. Hill had been close with the grieving family for weeks, and then had discovered that the blood was on the victim's husband's hands. Before the man could be brought into custody, he'd taken his own life. The reason was money – two lives cut short by bankruptcy.

'I don't want to look back on this job and remember that as my last case,' Hill told him with honesty.

Trying to lighten the mood, Hill put out his hand.

'And twenty quid says I'll have it wrapped up by the time you get back from watching the French kick your Welsh arses.'

'I suppose I could just sign it back from you next week,' Morgan conceded. 'And you can keep your twenty quid when you lose. Rugby's priceless.'

'Right then. You clear it with the guv and I'll get on my way to Hatton Garden.'

'Don't be shopping for Deb while you're on the clock, mind,' the Welshman laughed.

'Bit out of my price range,' Hill replied, smiling to himself.

# CHAPTER 4

**AS THE TUBE RATTLED** into King's Cross Underground station, Scowcroft raised his gaze from the carriage floor and met the eyes of Barrett amongst the other passengers.

This was their fourth and final station on the Underground, the multiple legs taken as a way to lose tails. As part of their escape, the trio had changed clothing in an alleyway with garments pulled from their backpacks. There, Charlotte had done what she could to clean up Barrett's battered face, but baby wipes and a baseball cap did little to hide the destruction of his nose.

'It's the London Underground,' Barrett had comforted his accomplices. 'No one points fingers or talks to strangers. I'll be fine.'

Hoping that he was right, they had boarded the westbound train from Chancery Lane to Bond Street. There they'd changed trains and lines for Waterloo, doing the same again to Leicester Square and then taking the Piccadilly line to King's Cross. Having emerged from the Underground, the thieves once again changed clothing in the mainline train station's public toilets. In the privacy of the stalls, secondary bags were pulled from within the original backpacks, which were then stuffed inside their replacements. Barrett had suggested that precaution, knowing that disposing of a bag in a train station was likely to raise an alarm in a city wary of terrorism.

Scowcroft stepped out onto the concourse and scanned the faces of those stood waiting for their trains. He saw nothing that raised his hackles. He looked over his shoulder, seeing Charlotte and Barrett in position behind him. He wasn't worried if they should lose him in the crowd – they both knew the rendezvous point.

He kept his head down, fitting in amongst dozens of commuters and tourists and looking at the phone in his hand. The screen was locked, but it was the perfect excuse to keep his face from the cameras. Behind him, Charlotte and Barrett did the same.

Scowcroft took an escalator up to the champagne bar. He waited there patiently until his two accomplices appeared on his shoulder. The trio was now complete, and aside from Barrett's nose, they resembled respectable tourists.

'I've got a reservation,' Scowcroft told the young hostess, who smiled at the handsome man in front of her as he gave a false name. 'Ashcroft. Sorry I'm a bit late.'

'That's no problem, Mr Ashcroft,' the hostess told him, pushing her hair back from her face. 'If you'd like to follow, I'll show you to your table.'

'Thank you,' he replied, wishing for a moment that he truly was an innocent tourist. His fantasy was cut short as he caught sight of the shock on the young woman's face when she took in Barrett's shattered nose.

'He's a cage fighter,' Scowcroft shot in quickly. 'We both are, except I'm a lot quicker than him.'

'Not too quick, I hope,' the hostess replied with a smile and swiftly left.

The table was at the English end of the champagne bar, and offered excellent views over the station below – if there was trouble, the thieves would see it coming. They all knew the location of the fire escapes, and their emergency rendezvous at St Pancras Gardens, but this was doing little to calm their fraying nerves as the adrenaline of that morning was being replaced by a bone-crushing weariness.

'Be nice if we could remember why we're here, instead of you trying to shag anything with a pulse,' Charlotte scolded Scowcroft as they took their seats.

'I know why I'm here,' he shot back, his mood shifting from arousal to anger in a split second. 'I'm here because Tony's my brother. I wasn't the one who tried to run out on him when he came back like he did.'

Charlotte's first retort died as an angry choke on her lips. The second was stalled by Barrett's intervention.

'Easy now, Alex. We're all here because we love Tony. Doesn't matter if it's by blood, marriage or mates. We're all here for him.'

'I'm not having her talk to me like that,' the young man grumbled, showing the immaturity behind his confident facade. 'You're not my family,' he told her, the words quiet but resonating.

'I'm *his* family,' Charlotte hissed. 'I'm his family, in a way you can't even imagine.'

'We'll see about that when he gets the full story,' Scowcroft told her. 'We'll see who's family when my brother wakes up.'

# CHAPTER 5

**HILL STEPPED OUT OF** the unmarked police BMW and looked at his shoes.

'Good start.' He smiled, his toecap poking into a patch of congealed blood. 'Now, where's the rest of it?' he mused, looking about him.

His eyes were drawn to the deep scratches in the pavement and scraps of rubber in the road, but there was no sign of how either had come about. Save for the patch of blood, there was nothing to indicate that a crime had taken place here only two hours ago.

Hill looked at the case notes Morgan had given him: a uniformed officer had arrived on the scene seventeen minutes after the call from a witness, but the report made no mention of any suspects or vehicles. The officer had initially written off the call-out as a hoax, but a second eyewitness came forward and corroborated the story of a street fight, seemingly over a bag. Hill searched the notes again, hoping he'd somehow missed the photos that the first responding officer should have taken. Finding none, Hill cursed the ineptitude of the constable.

Something had happened here, Hill was sure. But what?

He walked slowly to the address of the second eyewitness, scanning the pavement as he went. Besides some burnt rubber, there was nothing to draw his attention.

Hill pushed open a door and entered a glass-fronted coffee shop. The lunchtime rush was in full effect, and several queuing customers protested loudly as Hill eased his way to the front.

'Police,' he told the groaning line over his shoulder.

'Can I help you?' the shop's manager asked.

'Looking for Emma Pell,' Hill told her.

'She's one of my baristas,' the manager replied, pointing a finger towards a young woman who was frantically handing out fanciful concoctions of caffeine. 'You can't talk to her now. Look how busy we are.'

Hill smiled and pretended to care. 'Yeah, but you see, this badge says that I can.'

'Arse,' the manager muttered beneath her breath.

Hill joined the patrons waiting at the end of the long counter for their coffees.

'Emma,' he gently called to the barista.

'I don't have an order for Emma,' she replied without looking up.

'No, Emma, I'm Detective Inspector Hill. I've come to speak with you about what you saw today.'

'Oh!'

The girl looked to her manager for permission. The woman gave her assent with an angry nod, her eyes staring daggers at Hill.

'Take me to where you saw it happen,' Hill said, and Emma took him back out through the coffee shop's front door.

'It was down there,' she told him, pointing in the direction of Hill's BMW and the congealed patch of blood.

'And you were here when you saw it?'

'Yeah, I was just coming in for my shift and I heard the bikes, so I stayed to watch.'

'Bikes?'

'Motorbikes. They were riding down the pavement, heading straight at this group of people, and then it just turned into a massive fight.'

'How many people?' Hill pressed gently, taking notes.

'Three or four, and the two bikers. I thought it was some kind of TV thing at first, but then I didn't see any cameras so I guessed it was real. Was it?'

Hill resisted the temptation to tap the young woman's skull to see if it was hollow.

'It was real. Did you call the police?'

'I didn't,' the girl admitted, shifting her weight on her heels.

'That's OK,' Hill told her. 'Were you worried they might come after you if you did?'

'Nah, it's not that,' she laughed. 'I was using my phone to film it. Then I put it on Insta and Snap. I was gonna call the police when I'd finished, but by then you guys were already here so I just popped across to tell them what I saw.'

'And you gave them the video?' Hill asked, incredulous that this evidence hadn't been included in the case file.

'No,' the girl told him, her cheeks turning ruddy. 'I forgot.'

'But you remembered to put it on all of your social media?' Hill laughed, thinking about how much he was actually going to miss his job. 'You have it saved on your phone?'

The girl blushed a further red and shook her head. 'Deleted it. I don't have the space.'

'Don't worry about it, Emma,' Hill smiled. 'What's your Instagram account?'

# CHAPTER 6

**SCOWCROFT PUSHED OPEN THE** door to the champagne bar's bathroom. A sideways look in the mirrors confirmed that he had entered alone, his only company a rotund businessman wheezing at the urinal. Scowcroft dismissed him quickly as no threat and stepped into the stall.

The stall door stretched from floor to ceiling and fitted snugly. Scowcroft had the privacy he needed.

He opened the bag and pulled the crushed leather holdall from its depths. The bag's zippers were padlocked, so Scowcroft used his brother's commando dagger to cut through the leather. The blade had no struggle in cutting open the bag, spilling its bubble-wrapped contents onto the floor: a dozen golf-ball-sized packages.

He reached for the closest. A flick of the dagger was enough to cut the tape and open the wrapping like a flower. Seeing what was in his hand, Scowcroft's heart beat faster. He took hold of the next bundle and opened that, then the next, then the next, his heart beating faster all the time. Finally, he looked down at what was in his hands.

A dozen diamonds, and none below six carats. In the bathroom stall, Scowcroft held three million pounds' worth of precious stones.

But it was more than that.

Alex Scowcroft held his brother's life in his hands, and knowing that made him feel more powerful and more terrified than he ever had in his entire life.

For a fleeting second, an image pushed its way into the young man's mind of what could be. A life in the sun. Beach houses. Yachts. A never-ending supply of women of every shape and colour.

Scowcroft rejected the image. Better the family's terraced house with his brother than all of the superyachts and women in the world.

He placed the diamonds in a small leather pouch that was suspended from a chain that held two metal discs: his brother's dog tags. Then he wound duct tape about his chest to hold the small pouch securely in position. It created a visible lump under his T-shirt, but nothing that would be noticed beneath his winter jacket. Scowcroft took deep breaths to ensure that the tape would not restrict his breathing – he knew that they were not out of danger yet.

Finally, the diamond thief performed a solemn task.

His brother's commando dagger could not follow him on the final leg. Carrying such a weapon would draw unwanted attention from customs. So, after wiping it down thoroughly, Scowcroft reluctantly placed it into the walled cavity of the toilet's plumbing, vowing that he would return for the blade his brother had endured hell to earn.

Remembering to flush the toilet so as to avoid suspicion, Scowcroft left the bathroom and rejoined the others.

'I ditched his dagger,' he told them with sorrow.

'Never mind a bloody knife,' Charlotte replied, earning herself a scowl. 'What about the diamonds?'

'On my chest.'

'We're supposed to split them up,' she stated, trying to master her temper.

'They're on my chest,' Scowcroft said again, challenging her to struggle for them in the busy bar and doom their mission. 'I'll split them when we're closer to the target,' he pressed on. 'Our train's in forty minutes. We should go and clear passport control.'

'We've been talking about that, Alex,' Barrett interjected with calm. 'Something's really been bothering me, mate. I think we should let this train go and wait for the next one.'

'Why would we wait?' Scowcroft asked with a frown.

'The absence of the normal,' Barrett told him, then explained. 'Before me and Tony went to Iraq, they used to tell us to watch for the absence of the normal and the presence of the abnormal. In other words, you see something out of the ordinary, it probably means that bad stuff's gonna happen. And if you don't see something you should, that also means bad stuff's gonna happen.'

'What's that got to do with us, Baz? We're not in Iraq.'

'What was missing this morning, Alex?' Barrett posed.

'Police,' Scowcroft answered.

'Robbery and a street fight on Hatton Garden, and no police? I don't know why that is, mate, but it's definitely not normal.'

'And it's more than that,' Charlotte added. 'Those bikers were after the exact same thing we were.'

'Coincidence,' Scowcroft shrugged.

'Maybe,' she conceded. 'But then you look at the police not showing up, and it doesn't feel right.'

'It doesn't,' Barrett agreed. 'My gut tells me something is wrong here, Alex. I've had my eye on the news since we got here. Nothing. No stories. No coppers. There's another train in an hour and a half – let's just get that. We've come too far to half-arse this now.'

It wasn't in a Scowcroft's blood to sit and wait, and the youngest of the trio baulked at the thought. He may be outvoted, but he was the one with the diamonds.

Scowcroft wanted to leave now. He wanted to charge. He wanted to see this through and restore his brother's life not one minute later than he could. But he also knew that Barrett, a best friend to Tony since they were boy soldiers of seventeen, was the reason that his brother had been able to come home at all. Barrett's training and instincts had rescued Tony that day. Scowcroft hoped that those instincts would not fail them now.

'We wait an hour and a half,' he told them. 'And then we go to Amsterdam.'

# CHAPTER 7

HILL CONSIDERED SOCIAL MEDIA to be an essential part of any business, particularly in the fitness industry in which he was determined to thrive, so he was an active user of all platforms and earned a look of admiration from Emma as she received a follow request from Hill's Instagram account.

'You've got eleven thousand followers!' the barista said in awe. 'And amazing abs,' she cooed, scrolling through his pictures.

'Thanks, but let's concentrate on your video.'

They did, and what the detective saw astounded him – two motorbikes charging down a group of three pedestrians, who somehow turned the tables on their assailants and overpowered them. For reasons unclear in the video, the trio then bolted by foot, rather than using the van that Hill assumed was theirs.

'The tyres,' Hill said aloud, thinking of the scraps of rubber beside the blood. 'Someone slashed the tyres.'

Thanking Emma for her time, Hill took a moment to stand alone outside the coffee shop, his eyes working the length of Hatton Garden.

Two bikes, two riders and a van, all vanished. How? How was it possible to clear that carnage before the uniform had arrived on the scene? Neither Emma nor her video had been able to shed light on how or when the area had been cleared. She had been inside the coffee shop, busily uploading the video online.

Hoping the witness who'd called it in could help solve the puzzle, Hill walked along the pavement and found her in a jeweller's named Heavenly Diamonds.

'Mrs Underwood?' Hill asked a tall, nervous-looking woman in her sixties as the reinforced door closed heavily behind him.

'I am,' she replied, and seemed to brace herself as Hill held out his police identification.

'I believe you reported a crime, Mrs Underwood.'

'So what if she did?' a man's voice challenged from the back of the jeweller's.

Hill turned his head and caught sight of a grey-haired man he presumed to be her husband.

'Mr Underwood?' Hill asked.

'So what if she reported a crime?' the man asked again, ignoring Hill's question and taking a stand behind the thick glass counter. 'A fat lot of good it does.'

'What do you mean?' Hill posed, earning a contemptuous tut in reply.

'I mean, someone tries to do the right thing, and where does it get them? Don't bother to answer, and don't bother to ask any more questions either. My wife did her bit. How about you do yours?'

'I'm trying, Mr Underwood, but it would make my job a lot easier if I could talk with your wife.'

'No,' Mrs Underwood answered for herself.

'Well, OK then,' Hill conceded, knowing a brick wall when he saw one. 'I'm sorry to have taken up your time.'

He made for the door, but Mr Underwood wasn't done.

'You want to talk to someone about what happened, talk to that bastard across the street.'

Hill paused at the open door. 'And which bastard would that be, Mr Underwood?'

'Him,' the man spat, pointing a finger towards the opposite side of Hatton Garden. 'The owner of that sham.'

Hill followed the angry stare and read the jeweller's name above the tinted windows: Swiss Excellence.

An alarm bell rang in Hill's mind. A tripwire to a case five years ago, where a jeweller had loudly reported extortion and harassment, before finding himself face down in the Thames.

Hill turned back to the shop's owner, his tone lowered. 'You don't need to tell me anything, Mr Underwood. I believe I understand the predicament you're in. It would help me, however, if you could nod in the right places.'

After a few moments of thought, the man agreed with a look. He then unlocked the counter, placing several rings atop the glass. Hill played along with the ruse, pretending to inspect the jewellery.

'Swiss Excellence. That's now owned by Marcus Slate, isn't it?'

The older man nodded, though a tremor of fear made it seem more like a twitch.

'He bought it after the previous owner died?'

'Was bloody killed,' Underwood mumbled beneath his breath as he nodded, confirming the story that Hill had recalled.

'The fight today. It seemed to be over a bag. Did it come from that jeweller's?'

Another nod.

'I assume you have CCTV here. I don't have to take anything away with me, but could I watch it?'

This time the jeweller shook his head. 'You're not the first visitor we've had today, Inspector. All our hard drives have been taken.' His wife seemed to shrink at the memory.

'Someone came here before the police?' Hill asked, provoking a bitter laugh from the man.

'Before them?' Underwood spat.

Hill could see that the man knew he shouldn't talk, and was struggling to contain his words, but resentment drove them from his mouth.

'Let me rephrase that for you, Detective Inspector Hill. You're not the first *police* visitor we've had today.'

# CHAPTER 8

**HILL WAS SHOCKED BY** the accusation. In truth, he refused to believe it.

But then he visited the other jewellers whose CCTV may have covered the incident on the doorstep of Swiss Excellence. No one would talk. No one had footage which they'd hand over. In more than one instance, Hill saw a tremor of fear in the face of the shop owner as he announced himself as a police officer.

Finally, it was time for Hill to visit Swiss Excellence itself.

'How can I help you, sir?' a gentleman in a pinstriped suit welcomed him, putting forward a manicured hand in greeting.

Hill took it, enjoying the man's discomfort as he held his tongue.

'Sir?' the man finally managed, and Hill let go of the hand with a smile.

'Detective Inspector,' Hill stated. 'There was an incident outside here today, Mr . . . ?'

'Winston, Detective. There was? What kind of incident?' the man stammered, badly feigning shock.

'The kind that people like to cover up, it seems.' Hill smiled, catching Winston off guard with his directness. 'Why didn't you report the stolen diamonds?'

'What diamonds?' Winston protested, taking an involuntary step backwards.

'You were here this morning,' Hill asserted, closing on the man but still flashing brilliantly white teeth. 'We have your voice on the call,' he bluffed. 'Your call to Marcus Slate. You were telling *him* what had happened instead of the police.'

Hill had interviewed enough liars to read their eyes, and Winston's screamed that Hill had hit a hole-in-one.

'Listen, Winston, I'm not interested in who you tip off, or who you're laundering for. What I want to know is, who cleaned up that mess outside your window?'

Winston held his tongue. Then, as Hill inched his face closer, Winston saw something in the detective's eyes – it was the same single-minded drive that shone in the face of Marcus Slate, and Winston knew there was no option but to confess to this man.

And so he told Hill what he wanted to know.

# CHAPTER 9

**WITH TWENTY MINUTES UNTIL** the Eurostar's departure, it was time for the trio of diamond thieves to make their move.

'There's been nothing on the news,' Scowcroft confronted his accomplices. 'We got away with it, all right? Let's just get the train and meet Baz's buyer. I don't get what's wrong with you,' he pressed. 'Tony's relying on us. He's waiting on us.'

'Which is exactly why I don't want to mess this up, Alex,' Charlotte retorted. 'We went over every single possible scenario we could think of for this, but did we ever plan that there'd be a no-show from the police? We didn't. *That's* how strange it is. Something's going on here.'

'You're just nervous.'

'I'm cautious.'

'Well, what do you think, Baz?' Scowcroft pressed the gaunt-faced veteran.

It was a long time before he replied.

'Something that we don't know about is going on behind the scenes, but the fact is, we can't stay here for ever. I say we get the train and make for Amsterdam.'

'You see?' Scowcroft laughed, his bitter eyes on Charlotte.

'Hang on, Alex. I wasn't quite finished, mate,' Barrett told him gently. 'I think we should get the train, but divide the stones and split up. We can meet up again in Amsterdam, but at least this way, if something does happen, one of us should get through.'

'One of us is enough for Tony,' Charlotte agreed. 'We should go different ways. One on the train, one on the ferry and one flying.'

'Are you off your head?' Scowcroft yelled.

'Keep your voice down, mate,' Barrett warned the young man, seeing heads turn in their direction.

Scowcroft did lower the volume, but his tone was as harsh as ever as he laid into his brother's fiancée. 'You ran out on Tony with nothing,' he hissed. 'You think I trust you to stay when you've got a million quid's worth of diamonds in your pocket?'

Charlotte stood quickly and raised her right fist to bring it crashing into the side of the petulant boy's skull, but Barrett caught her wrist.

'Everyone calm down,' he urged. 'People are looking. Do you want to bollocks this up now?'

'Of course I don't,' Charlotte replied with heat.

'Alex?' Barrett asked, but was ignored. 'Alex?' he asked again.

But Scowcroft's attention had left the group, and the argument. Instead, his gaze was fixed on the escalators that carried patrons to the champagne bar.

And there, wearing a fresh suit and with his arm in a sling, was the big man that Scowcroft had stabbed only hours before.

Barrett and Charlotte followed the young man's gaze.

'Staircase,' Scowcroft told them. 'We all get the train, and we get it now.'

This time there were no arguments.

# CHAPTER 10

**IT TOOK HILL ONLY** two minutes to drive to Snow Hill police station, the location from where Police Constable Amy Roberts had responded to the call of the Hatton Garden incident.

'Why only her?' Hill pressed the stoat-faced desk sergeant.

'Wasn't a crime in progress, and we're on a tight budget. Big area to cover and not enough coppers. She was just there to take reports.'

'And where did she respond from?'

'Here, on foot. Budget,' the desk sergeant explained again.

'She arrived seventeen minutes after the witness called,' Hill said, his voice hard. 'It's a five-minute walk.'

The sergeant merely shrugged.

'Where can I find her now?' Hill asked, tiring of the silence.

'I can call her in.'

Hill shook his head.

'She's on her patrol route around the Stock Exchange area. You'll recognise her easy enough. Tall and blonde. Wasted in this uniform, to be honest. Sooner she gets a plain-clothes gig the better.'

Hill didn't bother to reply and left the station on foot.

The London Stock Exchange was close, and as Hill walked down Newgate Street he caught glimpses of the magnificent dome of St Paul's Cathedral between the buildings. Hill had been born and raised in the city, and the image of that cathedral standing tall amongst the fires of the Blitz had always provoked an intense pride within him. Now that his own grandparents were gone, it was almost as if the iconic architecture of the old city had taken their place as the guardians of Hill's heritage.

'Bugger it,' Hill thought aloud and took a side street towards the cathedral. He knew that starting a business would consume his time for months, perhaps years to come. When would he get the chance to sit and stare in awe at the striking lines and the subtle beauty of a place like St Paul's?

The case could wait twenty minutes.

Hill entered through Paternoster Square, taking his time to admire the space that so brilliantly trapped the autumn sun. Passing through a narrow archway, and squeezing by a group of eager Chinese tourists, Hill came out at the rear of the cathedral.

There was a cafe to his left and Hill took a seat, ordering coffee and a chicken sandwich. Then he pulled his headphones from his pocket, connected them to his phone, and opened an app that had become part of his daily ritual.

After years of training his body for optimal performance, Hill had finally been convinced by Deb of the need to train his mind. The app centred on a form of meditation known as mindfulness, the calm voice guiding Hill through his breathing exercises and helping him to put order into the scattered thoughts that bounced around inside his mind. In central London, a man with his eyes closed was not enough to draw attention or comment, and when Hill finished the seven-minute session, feeling revitalised and energised, a coffee and a sandwich sat in front of him.

But before he had reached for either he saw her.

PC Amy Roberts was on the opposite side of the square, giving directions to a pair of grinning backpackers. Thanking his luck that he wouldn't have to pace the area endlessly to find her, Hill picked up his lunch and walked towards the police constable.

As he drew near, and the backpackers went on their way, Hill saw that the desk sergeant had been right: Hill was six-two, and Roberts was easily his match. She was also strikingly beautiful.

'No wonder they all come to you for directions,' Hill smiled, then took a deep bite of his sandwich.

'Excuse me?' PC Roberts asked, her beautiful face drawing into the haughty mask that she used to drive away unwanted male attention.

'Don't worry about it,' Hill replied through a mouthful of bread and chicken.

'Can I help you, sir?' Roberts asked, forcing herself to add the title.

'Actually, you can,' Hill said, swallowing the mouthful. 'You can tell me how much they paid you to cover up the Hatton Garden robbery.'

Roberts froze, but her eyes widened in alarm.

'Are you a reporter?' she finally managed.

'Afraid not, Amy. I'm from Scotland Yard.' Hill dropped the words as casually as he tossed a corner of his sandwich to the pigeons. 'But I'm not with internal,' he added.

'Who the hell are you, then?' the constable asked, regaining some of her composure and fire.

'Well, that depends on what you tell me. I can be the guy who ends your career, and sees you do a nice stretch inside, or I can be the guy who conveniently forgets to include certain things in his report, and nobody cares because the case will be solved, and someone else will be going to prison. How's the second option sound to you?'

'Like I have a bloody choice. The same as I didn't have a choice this morning.'

'Go on.'

'Look at me. I can't blend in. I can't hide. They know where I am, and they know we patrol alone now since the cuts. Why do you think I'm standing in the middle of this sodding square giving directions?'

'Because you're scared,' Hill answered with empathy.

'Because I'm fucking terrified,' she hissed, her eyes backing up her words. 'They stopped me on my way there. Told me what I had to do.'

'And that was?'

'Turn a blind eye while they cleared the scene. There was no one there, just two bikes on the pavement and a van with slashed tyres. I had to wait for the tow trucks to come, and then they sent me to gather the CCTV.'

'Where's that now?'

'In the Thames, I'd imagine. One of them came with me, pre-tended to be a plain-clothes officer, but I could see that the owners of the stores knew better. There's a racket going on there, and they all know about it.'

'Marcus Slate?'

She shrugged. 'Maybe. There's been a big guy parading up Hatton Garden every morning. Catches a taxi from the end of the street. I saw him on my rounds a couple of times. I thought he looked out of place, a right thug in a nice suit, but then when I saw him come out of the shop that Slate owns, it made more sense.'

'What are they running out of there?'

'Diamonds, and I'm not going to die because two gangs were fighting over them.'

'How do you know it was diamonds?'

'It's Hatton Garden – what else can it be?'

'OK. Look, I understand why you did what you did. I know it's not black and white on the streets.'

Hill watched as Roberts balled her hands into angry fists, no doubt wishing she could take revenge on the men who'd threatened her and forced her to turn her back on the job and service that she no doubt loved.

'I feel like a piece of shit for it,' she said with anger. 'But these guys are serious, and I did what I had to do.'

Hill had nothing to say and simply handed her his card.

'I really hope you figure it all out,' Roberts told him, and Hill could feel her sincerity. 'But figure it out quickly, because someone's going to die for those diamonds.'

## CHAPTER 11

**SCOWCROFT PULLED A WEDGE** of twenty-pound notes from his pocket and waved them at the waiter to catch his attention, before dumping them on the table – the last thing the thieves needed was to be chased by the bar's security for running out without paying their bill.

'Follow me,' he told the others, and took them to the stairwell at the opposite end of the bar from the escalators, where the gorilla of a courier was now scanning the tables.

'How did he know where to find us?' Charlotte asked as they pushed through a fire escape. There was no alarm on the door, and the stairs led down into the main station.

'Not a question for now,' Barrett told her, his nose throbbing in agony as they bounced down the steps.

'There's the train,' Scowcroft told them as they reached the ground floor. 'Platform two. Don't split up too far, but don't walk in a bunch.'

The trio moved across the bustling concourse, Scowcroft resisting the urge to shoot a glance up at the champagne bar terrace. To keep his eyes rooted downwards, he pulled his phone from his pocket and pretended to type a text message.

'I don't see anyone else,' Barrett whispered as the men were pushed closer together through a turnstile and headed towards the passport checks of the French police. 'And they only saw *my* face. If it comes to it, I'll bolt and draw them away.'

'Bollocks to that,' Scowcroft hissed. 'They weren't the cops, Baz. If they get any of us we're done. No suicide missions.'

'If they see me, I'm running,' Barrett insisted.

'Fine, but me and Charlotte will run with you. That what you want?'

The thieves showed their passports to the French police officers and moved swiftly through to the platform, where they waited to board. Scowcroft was frustrated at being forced to stand in the open, but the press of other travellers about him gave him some measure of comfort. Reversing the camera on his phone, Scowcroft used it as a mirror to look over his shoulders. The action drew no attention from the other tourists, many of whom were taking selfies as they documented their travels, and Scowcroft saw no sign of the courier.

But he did see something else.

Twenty yards behind Scowcroft was a muscular, thickly bearded man in his thirties. He carried no baggage and appeared to be alone.

Perhaps these indicators alone Scowcroft could ignore. But why was the man looking up at the champagne bar?

'Baz. The stacked bearded guy behind us. I reckon he's with them. Where's Charlotte?' Scowcroft hissed, seeing no sign of her.

'She boarded,' Barrett explained. 'Next carriage.'

'Bollocks. We need to stick close.'

'Get into this one. We'll join her through the carriages.'

Scowcroft nodded, and the pair climbed aboard the Eurostar, Barrett pausing to help an elderly lady lift her baggage onto the rack.

'Thank you, dear,' she smiled. 'Oh! But what happened to your nose, you poor thing?'

'Bike accident, love,' Barrett grinned through missing teeth. He turned to Scowcroft. 'I didn't see the beard get on.'

'Must be waiting for his mate in the champagne bar. Where the hell's Charlotte?'

'Over here, boys,' the two men heard, finally spotting their female accomplice amongst a horde of lager-swigging men.

'This is Graham,' Charlotte explained, pointing to a slightly overweight man in his late thirties.

'Pleasure to meet you, lads,' Graham slurred, before remembering that he was dressed solely in a leopard-skin bikini. 'It's my stag do,' he added by way of explanation.

'Graham's been kind enough to invite us to join them for drinks,' Charlotte explained, having found an excellent way to disguise her and the other two for their journey.

'Yeah! Come get pissed with us, boys!'

Warm cans of lager were shoved into Scowcroft's and Barrett's hands, the men recognising quickly that there was safety and camouflage in numbers.

They pushed themselves into the throng of revellers.

'You got your dagger?' Scowcroft whispered.

'Dumped it with yours,' Barrett told him. 'There's glass bottles on that table if it comes to it.'

Scowcroft nodded. As a nineteen-year-old he had suffered a wound from a bottle himself and had the scars to remember it by.

'All right, then.' Scowcroft forced a smile, knowing their backs were against the wall. 'Cheers!'

# CHAPTER 12

**FROM BEHIND THE WHEEL** of his unmarked BMW, Hill hit speed dial, making his second call in as many minutes. This one was to his superior, Chief Inspector Vaughn. The first had been to the offices of Marcus Slate.

'You can't just go turning up at Marcus Slate's place, you idiot,' his boss told him on the phone, Hill picturing how Vaughn's freckled face would be pressed into his hairy hands.

'That's why I called ahead, boss.'

'You know what I mean, you arse. You've already got your redundancy. Why the hell are you pushing for disability on top of it?'

'So there are people above the law now, Chief Inspector? Is that what you're telling me?' Hill poked with levity.

'You know damn well that's not what I mean, but Slate has political clout as well as business. You rub him up the wrong way, Hill, and you can forget about ever opening a business in this city.'

'That thought had occurred to me,' Hill told him with honesty. 'But here's the thing, boss. I'm actually a big fan of Slate's. As far as British entrepreneurs go, he's up there with Branson.'

'You know damn well that Slate's not clean.'

'Ouch. I hope that wasn't deliberate, boss. And I'm not stupid, but I do want to meet the guy.'

'You're lucky it's your last week,' Vaughn told him, though there was no malice behind the threat. Like every superior officer Hill had served under since joining the force, Vaughn had nothing but good words to say about him.

'I know, boss, I know,' Hill placated. 'Now something's occurred to me about this robbery. Three of them bolted from the scene on foot. Can we pull footage from the local Tube and train stations? Say a half-hour window?'

'Yeah, I'll get the tech guys on it.'

'Cheers.'

'And you're sure this visit is just to blow smoke up Slate's backside?' Vaughn asked finally.

'Nothing but smoke,' Hill assured him.

'Well, I'll see you back at the office, then.'

'See you at the office, babe,' Hill replied, and cut off the call before Vaughn could berate him.

Ten minutes later, Hill pulled up outside the Chelsea property that served as the offices for Slate's business empire. The building was high-end but subtle. Like the man who owned it, the property hinted at money and power, but the secrets of its wealth were kept within. Slate was not an entrepreneur who was about to launch a podcast, hold seminars or write a memoir.

Hill had heard the rumours, but his admiration for good business had led him to study Slate's path to riches closely enough to separate the facts from the fiction. As he stepped out of the car, he prepared for the meeting by running through what he knew of Slate.

Growing up in London, Slate was the son of an East End mechanic. The story went that at fourteen Slate junior had dropped out of school and helped transform his father's failing business from a repair shop to a spare parts supplier. Within a year the business had been profitable. Within five, Slate had opened a further three sites across London. Within ten, he'd owned twelve nationally.

And then the Internet had become a part of everyday life, revolutionising the way people shopped. Twenty-four-year-old Slate had seen the future, and had been one of the first to offer spare car parts online. He'd bought out the competition, and three years later he'd made the *Forbes* list as one of Britain's wealthiest young men.

The story was inspirational: a young boy who rescued the family business and, with the vision few people possess, saw the way his industry would evolve in the future.

But that was only half the truth.

Slate had not dropped out of school – he had been expelled for repeatedly assaulting his fellow pupils and teachers. In the ten years before he'd opened his Internet stores and marketplaces, Slate had seen the inside of a courtroom on several charges. His final appearance, for grievous bodily harm, had earned Slate six months in prison. Ironically, it had been there that he learnt of the emerging possibilities of the Internet, taking all the IT courses available through the prison reform programmes.

As Hill stepped into the plush lobby of the mogul's office, he smiled at the thought that the taxpayer had given Slate the education and time to exploit such a gap in the market.

'Detective Hill,' he told the three beauties behind the desk. 'How many of you does it take to answer the phone?' he couldn't help but add, earning a smile from two and a look of contempt from the third.

'Mr Slate is expecting you. Please follow me,' the sour-faced secretary told him, her tone as sharp as her eyes.

They came to a pair of thick mahogany doors. Along the corridor, Hill saw two men sitting behind a desk that was home to only mugs of tea and a television. The muscular men gave him a dismissive look and turned back to their talk show.

'That the concierge, is it?' Hill asked the secretary.

She ignored the jest and knocked at the door.

'He's a very busy man, Detective, so please keep it short.'

'But of course,' Hill smiled, thick-skinned from years on the force. Compared to being spat at and beaten as a uniformed bobby, a few narrowed eyes and dismissive glances were no sweat.

Hill stepped into Slate's office, and the door clicked shut behind him. In the next instant, adrenaline and panic coursed through his body.

Because the room was empty.

# CHAPTER 13

**NOT A DESK. NOT** a chair. Not a single family photo. Save for the plastic sheeting on the floor, the room was completely empty.

Hill span on his heel, grabbing for the door handle.

It turned. It opened.

And Hill found himself staring into the face of Marcus Slate, who had something in his hand.

Tea.

'Hold the door then, mate. Sorry, Detective Inspector,' Slate corrected himself with a smile. Hill obliged after a pause to reset the chemical actions of his fight-or-flight defence.

'Sorry about the room,' Slate said. 'I'm a private person, Detective, and I can be a pretty messy one, so I don't like having people from outside of the business in my office where I have all kinds of documents lying about. I've just had this room redecorated, but we're still waiting on the furniture. Still, I'm glad to be on my feet and away from the desk for a change, if I'm honest with you. Here you go.' Slate handed Hill a mug.

'Thanks.'

'Soya milk and no sugar, right?' Slate smiled, and Hill's mouth dropped.

'Watching my figure,' Hill replied, hoping he didn't appear rattled.

'Yeah, I saw your Instagram. You're something of a fitness fanatic.' Slate's white teeth flashed like a wolf's. 'And you follow some interesting people, Detective.'

Hill tried to feign calm by sipping at the tea, but it did little to melt the ball of ice that was formed in his stomach.

'Some young lady on there. @emslondon, I think her username was. She had some really fascinating videos.'

'She did? Tea's great, by the way.'

'Isn't it? Sri Lankan. And yeah, she did. I'd show you, but looks like she deleted the account, which is a shame.'

Hill cursed himself for leaving a trail to Emma, his coffee-shop witness, then remembered that she had already been compromised by the actions of PC Roberts.

If Slate wanted to play the game, then Hill would oblige.

'People spend too much time on social media,' he told Slate. 'People don't talk any more, and that can be a problem. Lucky for me, I think of myself as a problem-solver.'

'Do you now?' Slate asked, feigning a smile.

'I used to love doing jigsaws as a kid, Mr Slate. My older brother liked to upset me by hiding the pieces around the house, but I'd hunt them down, one by one. When I got bigger, I stopped having to look for them.'

'Grew out of playing puzzles, did you?'

'No, Mr Slate, but instead of looking for the pieces my brother was hiding, I'd just beat them out of him.'

For a moment Slate had no retort. Behind the facade of calm, Hill knew the man's anger would be bubbling over. Police officer or not, he was walking a fine line.

'Diamonds, Mr Slate. Your diamonds, stolen this morning.'

'It's a crime to be a victim of crime, Detective?'

'No. But it's a piece of a puzzle. A large one. And when the pieces of this puzzle are put together, it's not going to be a steam train in the Scottish Highlands, Mr Slate. It's going to be a long stretch inside.'

Hill looked into Slate's eyes. There was danger in them, a lot of danger, but Hill had faced intimidation before and knew how to deal with it. Both men had made their threats with insinuation and subtlety, but now Hill sensed the moment to be direct.

'I'm going to expose your diamond heist,' Hill told the man who could have him killed. 'I'm going to expose you, Mr Slate, and then you're going to prison for a long, long time.'

# CHAPTER 14

**HILL SLUMPED INTO THE** driver's seat of his BMW.

'Fuck.' He exhaled heavily, his fingers tingling with adrenaline.

He sat there for a moment with the engine off, hands in his lap. He told himself the delay was to show Slate, who he was certain would be watching, the demeanour of an ice-cold detective. In truth, Hill didn't trust his shaking hands on the wheel. He had walked a very fine line, and he was lucky to still be in one piece.

In one piece for now, at least.

After a moment to catch his breath and steady his nerve, Hill pulled out of the automatic gate and into the Chelsea traffic.

Taking a few more deep breaths, and noting that the trembling was almost gone, he called his boss.

'How'd it go with your idol?' Vaughn asked.

'You know what they say about meeting your idols, boss.'

'I wouldn't know. Mine are Brian O'Driscoll and Rory McIlroy. Can't say we move in the same circles.'

'Slate set up his diamonds to be stolen,' Hill stated, getting to the point. 'They've been parading them outside the jeweller's he owns for weeks. One guy, one bag, no other security. The guy walks to the end of the street, gets a taxi, and comes back at the end of the day the same way.'

'And where's he going between those times?'

'Slate tells me it's to show the diamonds to prospective buyers. I've got a list.'

'And I'll bet a cross-check of them shows they're friends or associates of Mr Slate.'

'Exactly, boss.'

'So what's in this sham for him?' Vaughn mused.

'I'm guessing at the moment, but I think it's insurance.'

'Insurance? But what's the point in that if he loses the diamonds? He'd just be getting back the value of the stones he'd lost.'

'Not if *he* stole them,' Hill explained. 'Slate stages the robbery, keeps the diamonds, sells them on the black market, and gets the three million they're insured for. As far as the insurers are concerned, Slate's courier and jeweller were following the same pattern that had been safe every other day, and then got unlucky. What Slate didn't see happening was another gang spotting an easy meal, and swooping in before his own guys could.'

'Bloody hell,' Vaughn sighed. 'So who are this other lot, and where are they now?'

'I don't know, boss, but wherever they are, they're dead men walking.'

After exchanging goodbyes Hill hung up and began to type Scotland Yard into a traffic-beating app on his phone. He was about to hit enter when an incoming call flashed onto the screen – Vaughn.

'Boss?' Hill asked, puzzled.

'St Pancras station,' Vaughn told him, excitement in his voice. 'The techies pulled three faces from Chancery Lane Tube station and the three flashed again on the facial recognition software. They're at St Pancras.'

'Where are they going?' Hill asked, hitting a hard right turn.

'If they haven't left already, then there's one at the platform with a final destination of Amsterdam.'

'Amsterdam?' Hill replied. 'I can't think of a better place to offload the diamonds, can you?'

Vaughn couldn't. As with many of the city's vices, Amsterdam's thriving diamond trade had a reputation for turning a blind eye.

'Departure time?' Hill pushed.

'Forty minutes ago. Trouble in the Tunnel again. I've got uniforms on their way there now.'

'Tell them to wait for me.'

'You're on borrowed time, Hill.'

'I want to close this case, boss. Email me the shots of their faces.'

Hill hung up, then hit the blue lights and sirens that were concealed behind the BMW's grill.

He raced through central London's streets, his mind full of visions of how he could end his career in glory.

'Just stay where you are,' he prayed, and hoped the thieves would listen. 'Just stay where you are and make me a hero.'

# CHAPTER 15

SCOWCROFT FIDGETED IN HIS train seat and looked out the window. By now the train should have been inside the darkness of the Channel Tunnel, well on their way to Europe.

Instead, Scowcroft looked up at the magnificent wrought-iron ribs of St Pancras station's roof.

'Why the hell are we still here?' he hissed at Barrett beside him.

Barrett shrugged. 'Conductor says it's a problem on the line.'

'Here,' Charlotte spoke up, handing them her phone – it was showing the BBC News app. 'They've had refugees trying to get on the trains coming this way. Says that one of them's dead.'

'Well, how long will that hold us up?' Scowcroft pushed, but no one had an answer for him.

Surrounding the thieves, Graham's stag do were raucous, outlining in detail their hedonistic plans for Amsterdam and its red-light district.

'I'm gonna go take a piss,' Scowcroft told them, standing. 'See if there's any sight of the big lad or the beard.'

'Don't wander off,' Charlotte said, earning a contemptuous tut in reply.

Scowcroft left the carriage and tried the toilet door. It was locked, and sounds of retching came from within – the first casualty of the stag do.

He ran through the events of that morning in his mind. At no point had his face been revealed to the big man or the bikers, and he had been well clear of the scene before dumping his mask into the backpack. Of average height and build, Scowcroft was just one more twenty-something male in a city that held tens of thousands of them, so he considered it safe to walk the train. If he was on board, the courier was sure to be made conspicuous by his size. Likewise, the bearded man wouldn't blend in amongst the increasingly irritated businessmen and parties of tourists.

Scowcroft moved from one carriage to the next, finally coming to one that served as a dining carriage. Scowcroft bought half a dozen packets of sandwiches and bottles of water. The cost made him baulk, and then the young man laughed, remembering that three million pounds' worth of precious stones were taped to his chest.

'You can keep the change, love,' he told the server with a smile, and moved back to rejoin the others, the sound of the stag party reaching him long before he entered the carriage.

'Long time for a piss,' Charlotte snorted.

'I got these,' Scowcroft explained, dumping the bag into Charlotte's lap.

'Shit,' Barrett groaned.

'What? You don't like ham and cheese? It's all they had, mate. Bloody French.'

'No.' Barrett shook his head, his face turning pale. 'That.'

Scowcroft followed the man's gaze, and the bread turned to ash in his mouth.

Two British policemen appeared to be casually walking the platform, but with a soldier's instinct Barrett had recognised their fleeting glances at the train's windows, and the hands that rested ready on the hilts of their extendable batons.

'They're looking for us,' Barrett almost sighed.

'How can you be sure?' Charlotte pressed, desperate for him to be wrong.

'The insignia. Those aren't transport police. They're the Met.'

'Bollocks,' Scowcroft hissed. 'Over by the escalators. There's another one there. That must be why the big lad and his mate have done one.'

'They're putting the nets out,' Barrett assessed.

'So what do we do?' Charlotte asked.

'We get off the train,' Barrett answered, and Scowcroft nodded in agreement.

'But first . . .' the younger man said, tapping his chest to still their questions.

Scowcroft left the carriage and moved to the closest toilet. It was open, but splattered with vomit. The thief had no time to notice. The sight of the police had sent his heart beating fast against the stones. He knew the time had come to divide them. He took eight from the pouch, placing four in each of his trouser pockets. He was about to retape the remaining four to his chest, but another idea came to him.

Scowcroft would swallow the stones. If the big man and his friends were to catch him, then they'd have to gut him before Scowcroft failed his brother.

He swallowed, washing down the diamonds with handfuls of water from the washbasin.

'Here,' he told Charlotte and Barrett when he got back to their seats, handing them the diamonds beneath the table. 'Swallow them. Right now. Don't mess around.'

Neither did, knocking back the small rocks with bottles of water.

'Christ!' Charlotte gasped.

'Hey,' one of the stag party grinned, his voice conspiratorial. 'Is that Mandy?' he asked – meaning ecstasy.

'Travel sickness pills,' Scowcroft replied. 'Sorry, mate.'

'Oh,' the man said sadly, before his eyes brightened up. 'Guess I'll stick to the coke then.' The size of his grin suggested much of the powder had already been consumed.

'This is the best place you found for us to sit, yeah?' Scowcroft whispered to Charlotte.

'You don't have to be a Scowcroft to make a decision,' she replied. 'If trouble comes, you'll be glad I did. You'll see.'

'Wait. You feel that?' Barrett cut in, smiling. 'The table's vibrating! We're ready to go!' The conductor's whistles on the platform were closely followed by cheers from the stag party.

'Thank God,' Charlotte sighed, seeing the police making no effort to board. 'We're clear.'

She couldn't have known about the man entering the station, and how desperate he was to prove her wrong.

# CHAPTER 16

DETECTIVE INSPECTOR HILL SPRINTED across St Pancras station's concourse, the uniformed sergeant beside him struggling to match the pace.

'Can't they stop it?' Hill demanded of the man as the pair flashed identification at the border officials.

'We've got no cause, sir,' the sergeant told Hill for the third time. 'Three robbery suspects is not enough to hold an already delayed international train. We're not even sure they're on there.'

'They're on there,' Hill declared, trusting his gut and pushing his way through a group of startled tourists.

'Where are your officers? How many are on the train?'

'Well, none, sir,' the sergeant told him, fighting for air. 'They can't go to Europe.'

Hill swore beneath his breath, scanning the scene about him. Whistles rang along the platform. Hill knew the train's doors would close in a second, and with them his chances of catching the thieves.

'My car's pulled up across the front!' he shouted at the sergeant, tossing him the BMW's keys as he leapt through the open door and onto the train. The closing door cut off the sergeant's shocked reply.

'You can't do this, sir,' Hill lip-read. He smiled as he waved the man goodbye.

The train lurched forwards. There was no turning back now. Either he would come out of this a champion or a disgrace. He knew he was placing his redundancy package – and therefore the future of his business – in jeopardy, but Hill believed in bold strokes, and he trusted his gut. The thieves, and Slate's diamonds, were on this train.

After a few moments to collect his thoughts, Hill pulled out his phone.

'Now, don't get angry,' he said into it after Vaughn answered, 'but I'm on the Eurostar.'

'Yes, I just bloody heard from the sergeant! What the hell are you doing, Hill? Get yourself off there at the first stop. If you're lucky, maybe we can keep the IPCC out of this.'

'I'm going to Amsterdam, boss, but I'll be back tomorrow.'

'You've got no jurisdiction to operate on the Continent, you stupid git!'

'I know that, boss. That's why I'm calling you to let you know I'm taking tomorrow off as leave. Pretty sure I've got a couple of days left in the bank, and I was already pushing into overtime today. This is just an above-board day break across the Channel.'

'Right, but all that goes to shit when you find these thieves of yours.'

'Exactly. *When* I find them,' Hill smiled. 'These thieves scream amateur to me, boss, and they've bitten the hand of one of the shadiest men in London. If I don't find them before his crew does, then we'll have an international murder enquiry on our hands.'

'Christ. OK. I'll call ahead to a friend of mine in Amsterdam. I'll write it up as a familiarisation visit.'

'You're a good bobby, boss,' Hill told Vaughn, and meant it.

'Save the arse-kissing, Hill. Just find those thieves before they're corpses.'

# CHAPTER 17

**OPENING THE EMAIL VAUGHN** had sent him, Hill once again studied the faces of the three thieves he was tracking. State-of-the-art, anti-terror surveillance software had matched the images, but to a human eye the photo stills were distorted and blurry, and there was little Hill could gain from the photos except the knowledge that he was tracking two men and a woman. Luckily for him, he'd spent the last thirteen years of his life spotting people breaking the law, and he had come to recognise the signs. The thieves would make a mistake, or somehow show their hand, he was sure of it.

So Hill began a slow inspection through the carriages. He had to assume his suspects would have split up for the journey, so anyone who could match their description had to be studied. Hill knew the trio had been fit and able enough to beat off the attack of the bikers, so he kept his eyes peeled for healthy but potentially bruised individuals.

Hill's searching drew several comments from passengers, but the detective let them wash over him. He may be causing some slight offence, but he hoped he was doing nothing to attract the kind of attention that would jeopardise his search.

He was wrong.

'Sir?' A conductor stopped him in the passageway between carriages, the man's English accented by French. 'May I see your ticket, please?'

Hill's eyes were drawn through the glass door to where a rowdy stag do were bawling football chants.

'Sir?' the Frenchman pressed.

'I don't have one,' Hill confessed, reaching for his wallet. 'Amsterdam, please. One way.'

'Sir, I'm afraid you cannot purchase a ticket on board the train. You should not have been allowed to board without one. May I see your passport?'

'My passport?' Hill asked, incredulous. 'You don't have that authority.'

'Then please accompany me to the police officer at the front of the train, sir. They do.'

'*I* am a police officer.' Hill spoke quietly, discreetly showing his badge.

'Are you on duty?' the Frenchman asked.

'I'm not, no.'

'Then I must ask you to accompany me, sir. You will be required to pay a fine.'

At least comforted by the knowledge that his thieves had no way of leaving the train before him, and not wishing to cause a scene that could draw attention, Hill turned to follow the conductor.

Then, as he stepped out of the gangway connection, Hill heard the flushing of the toilet, and its door unlocked. With the overactive senses of an officer, Hill turned to look as a man emerged from within.

A man with a broken nose.

'All right,' the Englishman said, catching Hill's eye.

'All right,' Hill replied, attempting to control his compulsion to act.

He succeeded, and after an awkward pause the broken-nosed Englishman stepped into the stag party's carriage, and Hill stepped into the other. Then, losing the battle with his twitching muscles, Hill finally smiled.

Because he'd found his thieves.

# CHAPTER 18

'WAKE UP.' BARRETT PRODDED Scowcroft. 'Amsterdam.'

Scowcroft opened his eyes and saw the Amstel river – from which the city of Amsterdam takes its name – stretching out beside the tracks.

'You didn't sleep?' Scowcroft asked, rubbing at his eyes as the train slowed into the city centre rail hub of Centraal station.

'Kept my eye on things,' Barrett replied, not wanting to admit that he was rattled. Though he couldn't place a finger on what was bothering him, the tripwire of his veteran's instinct had been triggered. 'We're all good,' he said aloud to reassure himself.

The Eurostar came to a final stop and the stag party let loose a mighty roar that drowned out the bilingual tannoy announcements.

'About bloody time!' one of the party shouted. 'We're out of drink!'

'You coming with us?' another of the men slurred at Charlotte.

'Course I am, babe,' she smiled back, before whispering to her partners, 'We can use them as cover to leave the station. It'll be easy enough to ditch them outside.'

Barrett liked the idea, but Scowcroft kept silent, reluctant to admit that Charlotte had found them a brilliant disguise for their journey from London.

'Let's go!' shouted the best man, the bikini-clad groom draped over his shoulder.

The thieves followed, pressing themselves into the group. As they stepped onto the platform and Dutch soil, Charlotte and Barrett put on big smiles, acting every part the travelling British lager louts. Scowcroft scowled.

This was usual for him, the young man full of fire and bitterness, but at that moment Scowcroft scowled because of what he saw ahead of them.

Dutch police officers. A pair at every exit.

His heart beat faster.

'They can't be here for us,' Barrett whispered, keeping up his smile. 'Look who they're stopping.'

Scowcroft did, and saw that the police were stopping mainly young people in gaudy neon outfits.

'They're looking for drugs,' Charlotte assessed, relief in her voice.

'No.' Scowcroft shook his head. 'You don't bring drugs *into* Amsterdam. Even the bloody police have to know that. It's a cover, so they don't spook us.'

'It's not. Just be calm, mate. It's fine.' Barrett was trying to reassure the younger man, noticing the sweat beading on Scowcroft's forehead.

'I'm gonna do something,' Scowcroft suddenly declared.

'Alex, don't,' Barrett pleaded.

'Don't you fucking dare,' Charlotte hissed, her eyes ablaze.

But he did.

Scowcroft had already seen his chance – a loud-mouthed member of the stag party who was strutting along the platform as if he had bales of hay under his arms. Scowcroft moved forwards and shoved a businessman hard in the back, and the middle-aged man slammed into the drunken Brit, who spilled lager on his white trainers.

'Prick!' the lout shouted into the businessman's face, rounding on him and shunting him backwards.

The businessman tried to open his mouth, but before he could protest his innocence, the Brit threw what was left of his beer into the man's face. Then the businessman surprised even Scowcroft by replying with a quick right hook into the loudmouth's jaw, sending him reeling.

At that moment, the platform turned to anarchy as the rest of the stag party jumped on the businessman. The police were forced to bolt from their positions to intervene, leaving the thieves an open exit into the city.

They took it.

And at the end of the platform, one man watched it all.

# CHAPTER 19

**DETECTIVE INSPECTOR HILL HAD** been in no rush to leave the train. He'd seen the police waiting by the exits – why, he didn't know, but he wasn't about to question good luck – and he was certain his thieves would try to lose themselves in the crush of passengers.

So Hill had stepped from the train, walked to the back of the platform and made a call.

'Hello, babe.'

'I thought you were dead,' Deb replied. 'My phone hasn't been going off every two minutes. At least not from you, anyway,' she teased.

'That's because I don't want a horrific phone bill. I'm in Amsterdam.' Hill's eyes scanned the passengers that began to emerge from the train's doors.

'What? Why?'

'Calm down, Deb. I had to deliver some confidential docs.'

'You're not a bloody postman,' Deb moaned.

'I'll make it up to you,' Hill promised, eager to be off the phone before his wife's temper took over. 'Listen, babe, I've got to go, but I'll call you tomorrow, OK? Love you.'

'Love you too, but stay away from red lights, or I'll cut your bits off.'

Shaking his head, Hill hung up the phone and readied himself to move.

This was the time.

A steady flow of passengers were coming down the platform now. The police were searching the bags and persons of young adults, causing a bottleneck at the exits. Hill guessed the police action was an anti-drugs gesture, though why anyone would bring their own drugs with them to Amsterdam was beyond him. Doubtless a politician or high-ranking officer had thought it a great idea.

Hill now saw the stag party amongst the mix, the men launching into a lewd chant that Hill was well acquainted with from his rugby-playing days. Perhaps it was due to someone taking offence at the obscenities that a fight suddenly broke out, and in the space of one breath the platform turned into a mess of flying fists and chaos.

Then amongst all that chaos, Hill saw them.

He saw his thieves.

# CHAPTER 20

'LEG IT!' SCOWCROFT SHOUTED, grabbing his partners by the arms and tugging them clear of the melee. 'Come on!' he hustled as the police entered the fray. 'The exit's clear!'

'You stupid arse!' Charlotte chided him as they passed through the exit and onto the busy pavement.

'It worked, didn't it?' Scowcroft snarled.

'We should walk,' Barrett cut in. 'It's one thing running clear of a fight, but we should walk.'

Around them, other passengers who had run from the trouble had slowed their pace to breathless gaits. Amongst them, Barrett saw the old lady whose bags he'd helped place into the train's overhead storage.

'Are you all right, love?' he asked her, seeing her face was flushed. 'Come on, I'll carry your bags to the taxi for you.'

Scowcroft glared as the woman gave her thanks, but Barrett ignored his younger accomplice and turned to pick up the lady's suitcase.

And that's when he saw him – the man who'd looked into his eyes outside the toilet. The man who had studied his face, his broken nose. The man who, Barrett now knew, was the reason his soldier's survival instinct had been triggered. Whoever he was, the athletic man glided around the side of the melee at a slow trot, avoiding the flying fists and police batons with ease. Clear of the fight, he didn't slow down.

He was coming straight for them.

'I'm sorry, love!' Barrett shouted the apology as he hurled the woman's baggage into the man's path. It didn't collide with him, but it sent other travellers scattering. The fast-approaching man crashed into a young woman, sending them both sprawling to the ground, the woman crying out in pain.

'Go! Go!' Barrett shouted, but the others were already running.

Barrett chanced to look over his shoulder. He saw the man leap to his feet, unharmed, but the woman lay prone, and Barrett could see his pursuer was torn between tending to her and continuing his pursuit.

'He's police,' Barrett said as he caught up with the other two. 'He stopped to help that girl.'

Slowly, above their heavy breathing, the thieves became aware of the sound of bass and cheers in the distance. Mastering their temptation to run, the trio pushed off at a fast walk. The sound of music and cheering soon grew louder, as did the steady stream of ravers making their way in the direction of the party.

'What's going on?' Scowcroft asked a young girl whose face was painted with dots and swirls of neon.

'It's the Amsterdam Dance Event,' she told him in accented English that hinted at Italian. 'It's a five-day music conference, and party.'

'Outside?'

'Outside, inside – it's taking over the city.' She beamed at him.

Scowcroft smiled his thanks, and turned to his accomplices. 'How did we not know about this?' he hissed.

'We came here to sell diamonds, not to go clubbing,' Charlotte reminded him. 'Now make friends with that girl. Ask her to paint our faces.'

Scowcroft hated being told what to do by Charlotte, particularly when she was right, but the incident at the station had shaken him and the chasing man could still be on their heels.

'OK,' he relented.

Five minutes later, their faces painted neon and backpacks deposited into waste bins, the diamond thieves pushed their way into a crowd with their new friends, and were swallowed up by the party.

# CHAPTER 21

**'THEY GOT AWAY,' HILL** said into his phone. 'Bollocks!' he spat, hating to lose.

He was standing back from the streets that were a riot of noise and colour, the Amsterdam Dance Event in full swing. Hill was the only one present without a smile.

'Tell me you have a bone, boss,' he pleaded, pressing Vaughn for the reason that he'd called.

'I do,' Vaughn replied, and Hill could tell from his tone that his superior was becoming as invested in the case as he was. 'The CCTV images from the stations have come up with a hit on the facial recognition databases.'

'Well, that's bloody good news!' Hill beamed.

'Good and bad,' Vaughn admitted. 'One of them is Matthew Barrett. He served with the Commandos on three tours of Iraq, including the invasion. Made the rank of corporal, but was discharged for drug abuse a year after his final stint out there.'

'A Commando?' Hill asked, relishing the challenge. 'What did he do when he left? Any priors?'

'He's been living on welfare benefits since they kicked him out. The forces were his last employer.'

Vaughn paused. When he went on, Hill could hear the conflicting emotions in his voice.

'This was a good lad, before he went bad, Hill. Sounds like he's got balls enough for ten men, and if he was a Commando, he has the skills to back it up.'

'Don't worry about me, boss.' Hill grinned, looking out at the sea of partygoers. 'I know where he's hiding.'

# CHAPTER 22

**THE STREETS POUNDED WITH** sound and throbbed with the movement of thousands of ravers.

'They'll never find us in this,' Scowcroft shouted against the noise. 'It's insane,' he added with a smile, a young man after all.

'Head in the game, mate,' Barrett warned, attempting to bring Scowcroft back to earth. 'I'm gonna text the buyer.'

Scowcroft levelled out at the mention of the anonymous buyer. The search for a prospective customer for the stolen diamonds had been Barrett's child in the operation, and had involved months of feeling out old military contacts – men who made their living by selling their skills to the wealthy, the greedy and the crooked. To find such a connection took time and trust, but Barrett had finally found their go-between.

The connection was a former Commando known to Barrett from his deployment during the invasion of Iraq. The veteran – whom Barrett had sworn he would not name to his accomplices, or vice versa – had left the forces for the private sector, and was now bodyguard to an Arab prince. An Arab prince who coveted diamonds no matter their source, so long as the price was good.

Barrett had agreed to two million pounds for the dozen stones that were valued at three. The money would be enough for Tony, and that was all that mattered. Barrett hadn't turned to crime for his own benefit.

Now he took a cheap phone from his pocket and turned it on for the first time. Entering a number from memory, he sent a simple message: 'SEND.'

'Now what?' Scowcroft asked, the neon paint on his face doing little to disguise his anxiety.

'We wait, mate,' Barrett told him. 'Come on. Let's go find some food.' He led the trio into the narrow alleyways that ran from the densely packed streets.

'You want Charlie? Ecstasy?' they were asked by shady men in hoodies.

Scowcroft was wary of the criminals. 'They could be cops out to sting,' he whispered.

'Look at his eyes, mate,' Barrett schooled him. 'He's off his face.'

Partygoers came and went in the alleyways that fed the main party, but away from the crowds the group's camouflage was diminished.

'I'll keep a look up the street,' Charlotte volunteered, and Barrett led Scowcroft into a kebab shop with Arabic lettering on its sign.

'*Marhaba*,' Barrett greeted the greying owner, before going on to order the meals in the man's native language.

'Bloody hell,' Scowcroft said with admiration. 'I didn't know you could do that.'

Barrett shrugged. 'After the invasion, it wasn't a bad place for a while. We'd patrol around, get some food and some tea. It was all right, like,' he said, casually dismissing some of the most momentous times of his life.

'So why my brother?' Scowcroft asked, after a pause to catch his nerve.

It was longer still before Barrett replied.

'It all went to shit, Alex. Don't ask me the how and why, but it went to shit.'

The conversation was uncharted territory for the two men. Scowcroft had always yearned to know more about his brother's service, but the thought of Tony in his younger years, strong and vital, caused the younger man much pain to reflect on it.

As for Barrett, he had kept the memories of those days pushed down in his mind, weighted there by drugs, but the memory of his best friend would never let him be.

Perhaps it was seeing his brother's salvation at hand that let Scowcroft finally ask the questions that had burned inside him for almost a decade.

'Did he like it?' He pushed carefully. 'My bro. Did he like Iraq?'

'He loved it.' Barrett smiled. 'But he missed you. And he missed her,' he added with a nod towards the door. 'He never shut up about the pair of you.'

Their conversation was cut short as the restaurant owner placed their trays of food on the counter.

'Was he happy?' Scowcroft finally asked, taking great interest in the salt shaker. 'The day it happened. Was he happy?'

Scowcroft stole a glance out of the corner of his eye, and saw the older man's jaw twitch before he answered.

'Right up until that last moment.' The phone buzzed in his hand. 'Must be my guy.'

The message was from a Dutch number that Barrett had never seen before, doubtless bought to send that single text before it would be discarded: 'Get drinks with my British friend Pete at midnight. Table to the left of the DJ booth. Club Liquid.'

'We got our place,' Barrett said, taking his food from the counter and turning towards the door and Charlotte.

He was stopped by Scowcroft's hand.

The veteran met the young man's eyes.

'Thank you,' Scowcroft told him.

'It's just a kebab, mate.' Barrett attempted to laugh, uncomfortable with the admiration.

Then, as he turned away from the young man, Barrett wondered how Scowcroft would have thanked him had he known the truth.

That every day since the insurgent's bomb had blown their vehicle apart, Barrett had hated himself for saving the life of Tony Scowcroft.

# CHAPTER 23

'DETECTIVE INSPECTOR HILL?' HILL was asked by a Dutch giant of a man.

'That's me.'

'Sergeant Corsten. Please follow me and I'll show you to the control room.'

Hill followed behind the Dutchman's huge strides. They were in a mobile operations centre set up at a city-centre police station, the building providing a control point for the policing of the Amsterdam Dance Event.

'My chief tells me that you are here to see if there is something you can learn for the policing of festivals in London this summer?' Corsten asked, repeating the fabricated story that Vaughn and Hill had concocted.

'That's right, Sergeant. They get bigger every year, and the police force gets smaller.'

'Maybe that is why they send a detective to observe?' Corsten questioned with a knowing look.

Seeing that the sergeant had spotted the visit as a charade, Hill was content to smile and let him know he'd scored a point.

'Here is our CCTV room,' Corsten told him, pointing to banks of TV screens monitored by a mixture of police and private security personnel. From the look of a hard bearded man in the corner, even the Dutch special forces had their eyes on the event.

'Terrorism,' Corsten explained, catching Hill's gaze. 'But it makes our job easier, in a way. We wouldn't have half the number of these cameras and equipment if it wasn't for the terrorism budget. If you want to see the number of crimes prevented or responded to today, I can bring you the papers.'

'Sure.' Hill smiled, playing along. 'Until then, you mind if I take a seat? Oh, and do you have a Wi-Fi connection I can use?'

'Of course,' Corsten replied, and wrote out the memorised network and passcode for the detective before taking his leave. Hill didn't expect to see any paperwork. Corsten knew that Hill's familiarisation was a sham, but police officer to police officer, he was happy enough to look the other way.

Hill quickly cast his eyes over the TV monitors, seeing the same thing repeated over and over – DJs and revellers bouncing to a beat lost to the soundproofed control room. He knew that looking for individual faces in the sea of ravers without some direction was a pointless task. As he had on the train, Hill put his faith in the fact that the thieves would slip up, but this time Hill would not be denied his prize.

Connected to the Internet, Hill now opened up his phone's web browser and began to dig the thieves out from hiding with the one connection he had – the name of Matthew Barrett, and his service as a Royal Marine.

It was only moments before Hill had his first result. It was a BBC News article from 2008, listing Barrett as being awarded the Military Cross for his actions in Iraq the previous year. Further searches led to local news websites, where Barrett was lauded as a hero for saving the life of his hometown friend Tony Scowcroft, who'd been crippled in an explosion.

Now Hill had a second name, and he entered it into the search engine.

'Bloody hell,' he muttered, seeing a long list of results. All of them were fund-raising campaigns aimed at getting Tony the medical support he needed not only to recover, but to survive – his body was intact, but Tony was brain-damaged, seemingly beyond repair.

Scanning through the web pages, Hill saw that the latest plea had been posted on justgiving.com only three months ago, and aimed to raise the $2 million it would take for Tony to be accepted into a groundbreaking medical trial in America. If successful, it would give the man back his life.

But the campaign had raised barely $50,000.

'Bollocks,' Hill breathed, sitting back in his chair, because the reason behind the diamond heist had become abundantly clear, and the consequence of the thieves failing caused his stomach to turn.

'If I catch them, he's dead,' he whispered, and dropped his head into his hands.

# CHAPTER 24

**DEPOSITING THE LEFTOVERS OF** their takeaway meal into an alleyway bin, Scowcroft pressed Barrett for information on the buyer's location.

'He's told you twice already, Alex,' Charlotte cut in, her patience thin, but Barrett calmed her with a look and gestured to his smartphone.

'It says on here that it's a high-end club about a mile away, mate,' he told Scowcroft.

'What's high-end?'

'It means it's expensive,' Charlotte answered. 'It means we can't go in there dressed like this.' She gestured at their neon faces, jeans and trainers.

'Well, the bags are gone, and we're all out of clothes, so how the hell are we going to get into a place like that?'

'I'll look and see if there's a twenty-four-hour supermarket,' Charlotte proposed, taking out her phone. 'Are we expected at this guy's table?' she asked Barrett, who shrugged. 'It would help getting in if we are,' Charlotte told him.

'You seem to know a lot about this kind of club,' Scowcroft muttered, knowing that Blackpool's drinking and club culture was anything but high-end.

'I did have a life before your brother,' Charlotte replied without thinking, instantly regretting her words. 'I didn't mean it like—'

'Fuck you,' Scowcroft said, his voice flat and cold.

'I . . .' Charlotte tried to backtrack, but Scowcroft's eyes simmered with anger, and she knew it would be useless. Instead she concentrated on her phone.

'Here,' she pointed, her voice a shadow of its usual strength. 'We can get the clothes from there.'

Barrett knew Charlotte's words hadn't been meant literally, but even he was subdued at the implication in them.

'OK,' he finally uttered.

Charlotte moved to put her phone away, but an alert flashed onto its screen with a loud ping.

'It's the BBC News update,' she told them as she opened the app. And then she wished she hadn't.

Because Barrett's face was spread across her screen.

# CHAPTER 25

**IN THE POLICE CONTROL** centre's CCTV room, Detective Inspector Hill's guts churned as he watched over the monitors.

'Are you hungry?' Sergeant Corsten asked, noticing Hill's hand on his stomach.

Hill told him he wasn't and moved the hand away. In truth he was sick. Sick at the implications that his own success would have on a man who'd been crippled and brain-damaged while serving his country.

He rubbed at his eyes and tried to visualise a future where his decisions would concern buying a new piece of gym equipment, and not the life-and-death struggle of a brave man.

The detective's phone buzzed, and he saw the message from Vaughn: 'BBC just ran Barrett's picture.'

Hill opened the BBC News app, seeing that the newly released story was one of the top trending items on the site. He scanned the short article, which simply stated that Matthew Barrett, a former Royal Marine, was wanted in connection with a violent crime, and that his nose was badly broken. Above the text, the proud photograph from Barrett's military record sat alongside the grainy image from London's Underground.

The article was light on detail, but that was how Hill had wanted it. The news report was the beater that would flush Barrett and his friends into the open, he was sure of it.

'Look at this.' Hill heard Corsten address him on the second attempt, the Dutchman pointing a finger towards the room's CCTV screens.

Hill stood and let out a deep breath to clear his mind.

'Here,' Corsten jabbed with his index finger. 'And here.'

Hill followed the finger and saw what the eagle-eyed Dutchman had seen.

Something wasn't right in the colourful pictures of ravers. Two men – no, three – were combing their way through one of the stage's crowds, their thick shoulders and shaven heads marking them out as obviously as a tractor cutting through a field of hay.

'They are not there for the party,' Corsten observed, and Hill found himself nodding in agreement.

'You mind if I use your bathroom?' he asked.

'Of course.' The Dutchman smiled, knowing that Hill would not be coming back.

# CHAPTER 26

**BARRETT LOOKED INTO THE** faces of Scowcroft and Charlotte. Their wide eyes reminded him of his battle-shocked comrades in Iraq.

'You can't go,' Scowcroft finally murmured.

'Of course I can.' His mentor smiled. 'I'm not charging an enemy machine gun, mate, I'm just going to draw the police away from you two. Just remember, the buyer doesn't know you, or your names. You may have to win him over. Show him the news article. Here, give me one of your phones.'

Charlotte handed him hers, and Barrett flipped the phone's camera so that the screen showed himself and his two sullen accomplices. 'These two are with me, mate. You don't need to know who they are, and they don't know who you are. Deal with them. Out.'

'Pete's not his real name?' Scowcroft mumbled.

'No real names.' Barrett shook his head.

'Where will you go?' Charlotte asked, beginning to accept the inevitable.

'Your meet with the buyer is at the top end of the city centre. It's mostly waterways to the east, so I'll go south or west. I'll find a way of letting them see me, but keep enough cover that they can't catch me.'

'Baz,' Scowcroft pleaded, 'you'll go to prison.'

A genuine smile broke across the veteran's features. He couldn't tell his partners how his mind had been imprisoned and tormented since the moment he'd seen Tony's mangled body by an Iraqi roadside. He couldn't tell them that the four walls of a cell would be heaven to him, if only he knew that his best friend was restored.

'Since they kicked me out of the Marines, I've been living in shitholes worse than I ever did in Iraq,' he told them instead. 'I'll have a roof over my head, and food. I'll even have a gym.' Barrett smiled.

'We can't let you go,' Scowcroft insisted.

'Don't worry about it, Alex. I'll probably even run into some of the old unit inside. God knows they're in and out of the system enough. Just think of it as me being back in the barracks at Taunton, but no marching, and no pay.'

'You're a knob,' Scowcroft managed, trying to put on a brave face.

'Here.' Barrett pushed something into the young man's hand.

'Your diamonds?' Scowcroft said, shocked.

'I didn't swallow them. I got spooked on the train. I thought it would come to this, eventually. My good looks make me stand out too much.'

'Stop trying to make jokes and give me a hug, Matthew,' Charlotte told him suddenly, pulling her friend into a tight embrace.

At the display of affection, Scowcroft swallowed the ice-like lump in his throat. No Scowcroft was known for voicing their emotions, as Barrett and Charlotte well knew, but the young man tried his best.

'Baz,' he began, 'I'm not a soldier, but I'd take a bullet for you. I know you're Tony's brother as much as I am.'

Barrett simply nodded, not trusting himself to speak. Instead, he put out his hand. Scowcroft took it, his grip like a vice.

There was only one thing left to say.

'Good luck,' Scowcroft told him.

And Barrett walked away. When he had put some space between himself and his two friends, he tossed his cap down onto the pavement and lifted his face up to Amsterdam's camera-filled streets.

# CHAPTER 27

**HILL STEPPED OUT OF** the police control centre, but was stopped instantly by a commanding voice.

'Detective Inspector Hill!' He turned to see Sergeant Corsten approaching. With a sinking feeling, Hill considered that he'd misjudged the man.

He hadn't.

'Here's my number,' Corsten told him, handing over a piece of paper.

Hill's eyebrow rose in question.

'My priority is the safety of the people here,' Corsten explained. 'Including you, and whoever it is you're looking for. Who those men are looking for,' he guessed with a veteran officer's insight.

Hill paused before his next move. He could see no reason why the Dutchman would set him up to fail, or to fall foul of the local police force, and so he took his phone from his pocket and entered the number, texting Corsten a link to the BBC News article and Barrett's pictures.

'I need to find this man, and take him quietly home before somebody gets hurt,' Hill told him.

'Is he a threat?'

Hill shook his head without needing to think. All the evidence suggested that Barrett was a brave and selfless man. His actions may have been illegal, but they were noble.

'The people looking for him are,' he added.

Corsten gave a curt nod of acknowledgement and turned back to the control centre. Hill saw the ebbing tide of ravers coming to and from the stage, and followed his ears in the direction of the driving bass.

'Trance stage?' Hill shouted. A blank-faced steward pointed lazily ahead.

Hill pushed on through the crowd, and was funnelled into a circus-sized tent, his senses overloaded as soon as he set foot within. Lasers and lights criss-crossed the air above the hands of a thousand joyous clubbers.

At the far end of the tent stood the main stage, where the image of a leather-jacket-clad DJ was cast up onto a huge array of screens.

'Amsterdam!' the DJ's British voice came across the twenty-foot speaker stacks. 'Make some fucking noise!' The crowd replied with a roar that fought to drown out the drop of a pounding bassline.

Hill held his position at the rear of the tent and cast his eyes over the mass of bodies ahead of him. The thousands of moving limbs and the flashing light made it almost impossible to make out detail, and he wondered how he would find his target.

He pulled out his phone, and texted Corsten: 'Anything?'

The reply was instant: 'No sign of your man. I see you.'

Hill quickly texted back: 'What about the men looking in the crowd? Where are they?'

This time there was a slight delay, and Hill ground his teeth as he waited impatiently, praying that the men had not slipped away. 'Push down the left-hand side as you face the DJ. Thirty metres. Big guy on the edge there. Alone. Not dancing. Seems to be watching.'

Hill kept his phone in his hands and followed the instructions, spotting the man when he was ten metres away. Hill could see that he was a formidable build, muscular and bearded. The man seemed to be taking no interest in the music, only the crowd.

He remembered the bearded man in the police control centre and texted: 'You sure he's not one of yours? Special forces?'

There was a pause, where Corsten must have checked with the soldier, then: 'Not ours.'

Hill didn't move any closer, but kept the man in his sight. The detective was certain that Slate would have more men scouring the event. Having been burned once by the thieves, Slate's men would surely call in reinforcements before springing their attack, and so Hill would watch this man, and let him lead the way.

'I wanna see every one of your hands up!' the DJ called, the crowd cheering themselves as their fingers reached for the sweeping lasers.

And not wanting to give himself away to Slate's henchmen, Hill threw his own hands up with them.

# CHAPTER 28

**BARRETT STOPPED BESIDE A** canal to get his bearings. Taking stock of his surroundings, and seeing that the locals outweighed the few ravers, he decided that he had found himself in the no-man's-land between stages of the Dance Event.

The ex-Commando knew that his part in the heist was drawing to an end, but Barrett intended pulling the police into as long a chase as possible. Out here on the quiet streets, hemmed in by canals and tightly packed properties, he was a sitting duck.

He walked up to a Scandinavian-looking couple worn out from a day of drugs and dancing. 'Excuse me. Do you speak English?'

'Sure,' the man replied enthusiastically.

'Are there any stages around here?' Barrett asked.

'Right down the street, man. The trance stage. It's banging!'

'Thanks. What time does it finish?'

'Like, six?' the man guessed.

Barrett thanked him as he went on his way and began formulating a simple plan – he would lead the police to the stage and lose himself in the crowd. Should he evade them until dawn, he would slip out with the masses and attempt to take public transport to Belgium. If the police picked him up via their CCTV network – and Barrett hoped they would – then the press of bodies at the stage would give him the best chance for prolonging the chase.

He found the trance stage easily enough and entered to see a British DJ jumping up and down on top of the booth, exhorting the crowd to new levels of energy.

Seeing the smoke and flashing lights, Barrett was sure the crowd would make a maze in which the police would have to follow, but before he could let himself be swallowed by its depths, he turned his head up to the gloom of the canvas and hoped the police were watching.

Someone was.

Barrett saw him coming from his left, his soldier's instinct registering the man travelling at an angle that was opposed to the other ravers, who pushed as one towards the DJ at the head of the tent.

Barrett swore, plunging into the crowd and wishing he had more time. He pushed and weaved his way into the densest section of the dance floor, any chance of keeping track of his pursuers lost amongst the raised hands and writhing bodies.

Then, as if a giant switch had been thrown, all light and music was cut away, the stage cast into a pitch-darkness that was pierced only by the whistles and shouts of the crowd.

'Do you want more?' the DJ's voice echoed in the blackness.

The crowd roared that they did. Barrett prayed silently that his eyesight would adjust quickly to the dark.

'Do you want more?' the DJ screamed again, and the crowd matched his intensity.

'Then let's fucking go!' the DJ boomed, and the bass pounded through Barrett's chest, the lights coming up like a solar flare.

And in that flash of light, Barrett saw that his pursuers were almost on top of him.

As the music blared and the DJ hosed the crowd with champagne, Barrett pushed and shoved his way forwards, finally hitting the railing at the front of the stage. He thought to leap it but saw a line of security between himself and the DJ booth, so he followed it to his left, bumping and bouncing off the ravers. The drunk clubbers berated him, the drugged ones ignored him, but Barrett had no time to think about either and he finally came loose of the bodies in the giant tent's corner.

And there he saw a fire exit.

Barrett ran for it, ignoring the steward who called on him to stop, and barrelled out into the cold October air. He kept running, and heard more calls behind him – the police were on his heels.

The veteran turned right, seeing an assembly of artist and production trailers at the rear of the domed stage. What he didn't see were the thick cables running to and from them, and as Barrett chanced to look back over his shoulder, it was these that ended his flight.

He tumbled to the tarmac, feeling the skin scrape from his cheek and elbows. After a split second the agony of his already ruined nose began anew, but Barrett had no time to reflect on his pain.

Rough hands gripped him by the throat.

He was caught.

# CHAPTER 29

**A SUBDUED SCOWCROFT AND** Charlotte walked out of the twenty-four-hour supermarket, a bagful of fresh clothing in each of their hands.

'We need somewhere to change,' the young man said. 'There's portaloos around the raves. We can ditch our old stuff in them too.'

Charlotte shook her head. 'I need light and a mirror for my make-up,' she told him, and caught the young man's look of frustration. 'It's a high-end club, Alex. If we're going to fit in, I need to look the part.'

Scowcroft relented with a shrug, and pointed out a nearby hotel. 'Let's try that.'

They did, but the city centre hotel was fully booked. So were the next four they tried.

'We're running out of time,' Scowcroft grumbled. 'I can change in the street and go in alone.'

'They won't let a young guy in on his own. That kind of place, you need a one-to-one ratio at least.'

'Ratio of what?'

'Women to men,' Charlotte explained. 'Guys don't pay five hundred quid a bottle to be surrounded by other men. Besides, I have an idea.'

That idea led them to a part of the city where the windows pulsed with red light and the silhouettes of writhing bodies.

'Over here,' Charlotte instructed the wide-eyed Scowcroft, leading him through the door of one of the more decrepit-looking brothels. Scowcroft was assaulted by the scent of bleach and cheap perfume.

'Hello.' Charlotte smiled at the establishment's madam. 'I'd like a girl please, and he'd like to watch.'

The woman didn't bat an eyelid at the request.

'One hundred euros.'

'OK,' Charlotte agreed. 'And I'd like a woman, not a young girl.'

The madam shrugged and led them into a corridor washed with red light.

'What are you doing?' Scowcroft hissed into Charlotte's ear.

'Trust me, Alex.'

The madam pulled aside a heavy curtain, and the pair entered a shoebox that was home to a single bed, a toilet and a shower cubicle.

'In there.' She pointed first at Scowcroft and then at the shower.

'OK,' he stammered as the madam slid the curtain closed behind them.

A moment later, a curvy brunette glided her way in through the fabric, the cracks around her eyes deepening as she smiled an introduction. 'I'm Eva,' she whispered.

'Eva, I'm Charlotte.' The thief pushed a thick wedge of euros into the prostitute's hand. 'We need this room.'

Eva needed no more explanation. 'Anything you want,' she cooed, sitting down on the bed and groaning in mock pleasure as she counted her windfall.

'This is so messed up,' Scowcroft said, shaking his head.

'It's about to get worse,' Charlotte told him, pushing a small bottle into his palm.

Scowcroft looked at the label.

'Laxative?' he asked, shocked.

'Unless you want to cut the diamonds out,' Charlotte answered plainly. 'Put your T-shirt in the toilet bowl. Come on, don't make this any worse than it has to be.'

The next few minutes were a low point in the lives of the thieves. Save for a wry smile between moans, the prostitute appeared unmoved. No doubt she assumed the pair were drug mules.

Grateful for the presence of a shower, Scowcroft changed quickly, at all times keeping his back to Charlotte – he did not want to catch a glimpse of his brother's fiancée, no matter what intimacy he had just been privy too.

Pulling on a dark dress, Charlotte cast her eyes over her accomplice, approving of his well-fitted grey suit.

'Beautiful.' The prostitute beamed her own approval, as Scowcroft carefully pulled a coat over his shoulders – Barrett's diamonds rested within its thick pockets.

'Whatever happens, don't let me forget my coat.' He tried to smile.

'How do I look?' Charlotte asked him, finishing her make-up.

'Amazing,' he said honestly, before he could catch himself.

The pair weakly smiled their thanks to the prostitute, who stopped her moaning and pushed the money into the depths of her corset.

'Have fun.' She waved as Charlotte and Scowcroft slipped out of the brothel and onto the street, Charlotte's heels ringing on the cobblestones. The air coming off the canal was tinged with ice, and Scowcroft pulled his coat across his body.

'All right, love?' a drunk British tourist slurred at Charlotte. 'How much for a go around?'

'Hold my hand,' Scowcroft told Charlotte, surprising her. 'If they think I'm with you, they won't bother. We can't afford to draw attention.'

Charlotte took his hand.

'I'm worried about Baz,' she confessed.

'Me too,' he replied. 'Since what happened to Tony, he's been like my brother. I only just realised that today.'

'We'll see him soon,' she said, though she didn't quite believe it herself.

'I hope so,' Scowcroft breathed, then surprised Charlotte by coming to a stop, his hand like a vice on hers.

'I've got to ask you something.' His voice became hard again. 'Before this last bit, I've got to ask you. I've got to know.'

'Go on then.' Charlotte had been expecting this question.

'My brother. Did you want to leave him?'

'Yes,' she said without hesitation. 'Yes, I did, Alex.' She broke into a flood of tears.

Despite her words, despite his once furious anger towards her, Scowcroft pulled Charlotte close, his own tears coming.

'Why?' he sobbed. 'Why would you leave my brother?'

It was a minute before she could speak, but eventually Charlotte mastered her emotions.

'It wasn't after he got hurt,' she told him. 'It was before that. All the deployments. All the worry. All the stress. It was too much, for both of us. It was too much, but he was in love with the Marines as much as he was with me. I knew he'd never leave it. And so one day I told myself it was over, but I wouldn't tell Tony until he was back in the UK and safe. I didn't want that in his head if . . . if . . .'

'If the worst happened,' Scowcroft finished for her.

'And I feel like a bitch. It wasn't until I saw him in that hospital that I knew I'd wait for him for ever if I had to, through a million wars, but by then it was too late, and he's never going to know.'

As Charlotte's tears began anew, Scowcroft pulled her closer.

'He's going to know, Charlotte. Because of what we're doing right now, he's going to know. Tony's going to get his life back.'

# CHAPTER 30

**BARRETT'S WORLD WAS BLACK.**

A hood had been pulled over his head and the former Commando recognised the dank, musty smell of wet hessian. It was a sandbag that was hiding his captors from his eyes, and Barrett could almost laugh at the irony that he'd pulled the same bags over the heads of dozens of Iraqi men.

But Barrett wasn't laughing.

He was scared.

Since when did the police hood the men they arrested? Could it be that he'd somehow fallen foul of an anti-terror operation?

Perhaps Barrett would get his answers, because suddenly the hood was whipped away, his eyes quickly adjusting to what appeared to be the gloomy interior of a van. There was no sign of his captors. He tried to turn, but his feet were in shackles, his hands tightly bound behind his back.

He became aware of a presence behind him. He could hear the man's breathing. Minutes passed while Barrett waited for his captor to say something or make his move. Finally, he felt compelled to fill the eerie void.

'Look, I know we broke the law, all right? But you can't go tying me up like this. You're violating my rights.'

Silence.

'Don't you want to ask me anything? I'll talk. I'll tell you about how we got forced to do this, because the government won't look after its own. How it bleeds its soldiers for oil, then throws them away when they're broken. I'll tell you about that!' Barrett was shouting, his anger and bitterness growing.

His captor still said nothing.

'What would you do if your partner was put in coma, and your government just left him to rot? Well? You're a police officer – you think that's justice?'

And then Barrett felt the presence of the man lean in from behind him, his words a chilling whisper against the captive's ear. 'I'm not a police officer.'

# CHAPTER 31

**'IT'S ALMOST TIME,' SCOWCROFT** told Charlotte, looking at his watch as if mesmerised by the passing seconds.

The pair stood on the street opposite the entrance to Club Liquid. A line of would-be patrons stretched back along the block. When the doors opened to admit the lucky few, the pounding of house music pumped out from within.

Charlotte ran her eye over the line, seeing well-heeled twenty-somethings. It was certainly a different crowd to the street parties taking place at the Dance Event.

'We should go in,' Scowcroft said. She followed alongside as they headed directly for the door, bypassing the line.

'We're at Pete's table,' Scowcroft told the beautiful hostess, who looked the pair up and down.

'OK,' the local shrugged after a moment, her eyes lingering on Scowcroft's handsome face. 'You can both come in, but tell Pete no more guys.'

'Sure,' Scowcroft answered, and smiled his thanks at the colossal bouncer who held open the door.

Inside, the pair were accosted by the throb and blare of music. The dance floor was a tangle of bodies, but Scowcroft's eyes were drawn to the sectioned-off tables that ran along its edges. There, the most beautiful women in the club danced with each other, the men at the table content to sit back and watch, safe in the knowledge that their connections or wealth would see at least one of the girls going home with them.

Scowcroft again had a vision of what could be with the diamonds in his possession. It could be him buying tables at high-end nightclubs. Him surrounded by beautiful women.

But no – Scowcroft only wanted to be surrounded by his family. Tony, Barrett and, as he looked at her beside him, even Charlotte.

Even Charlotte. If nothing else came from this whole endeavour, at least Scowcroft could take comfort that his brother was adored.

'You should wait here,' he told her, suddenly protective. 'I'll go to the table with the diamonds.'

'We're both going,' Charlotte replied, calmly but firmly.

'What if it's a sting? They're going to catch Barrett, Charlotte. If they catch us too, then who's left for Tony?'

'What choice do we have?' she said plainly. 'This is it. It's all or nothing.'

Scowcroft knew she was right.

All or nothing.

'Then let's do it.'

# CHAPTER 32

**THE BUYER'S TABLE WAS** easy enough to find, sitting in the prominent position to the left of the DJ box, the single man sat behind it swarmed by half a dozen beautiful women.

'I thought the girl at the door said no more men to this table?' Scowcroft shouted above the noise of the music.

Charlotte shrugged in reply. 'I guess they left.'

'Or they gave us the wrong place to meet.'

'They didn't,' she told him, and prayed that she was right. 'Just look like you belong.' They cut along the edge of the dance floor and towards the front of the club.

'Hi.' Charlotte smiled at the bouncer watching over the table, breezing straight by him up the couple of steps to the table that allowed the people at it to see – and more importantly, be seen from – anywhere in the club.

'Pete?' Scowcroft asked the lone man on the couch.

'That's me,' he answered in a British accent. 'Girls, give us some space.' Scowcroft was intoxicated by their perfume as they wafted past him and down the steps.

'Take a seat,' the man offered, and Scowcroft obliged. Pete was a handsome, athletic-looking man in his thirties. He looked every bit how Scowcroft expected a former Commando turned lucrative contactor to appear.

'Where's Baz?' Pete asked.

'Broken nose. Didn't think it would be a good idea to draw attention,' Scowcroft answered. 'He gave us a video.'

Pete smiled and waved the gesture of the footage away.

'I saw the news. I'd told the staff on the door not to let him in. At least this way I won't have hurt his feelings. Drink?'

Scowcroft shrugged in answer, and Pete gestured to a server. The stocking-clad blonde poured four large vodkas.

'I'll take Baz's,' the buyer told them. 'To those who can't raise a glass.'

The three of them knocked back the vodkas.

'Another one?' Pete asked. 'It goes for ten grand a bottle here, so enjoy it.'

'Business first.' Charlotte smiled. 'It's been a long day, Pete.'

'Of course it has,' the man allowed, doubtless no stranger to long days himself. 'Let's go over it, then. My car and driver are outside. The money, for obvious reasons, is in there.'

'We're not driving anywhere to do it,' Scowcroft cut in, his voice calm but forceful.

'Of course not.' Pete shook his head. 'My driver will get out. As a measure of trust, one of you can get behind the wheel. The other will get in the back with me, where we can inspect the goods. Once we're both happy, you guys get out with the money, I come back in here to the company of these beautiful ladies, and the driver takes the stones to my employer. Sound good?'

'Works for us,' Scowcroft announced after sharing a look with Charlotte. 'Thanks for meeting with us.'

'Not a problem. Anything for a good cause.' The man beamed.

'A good cause?' Scowcroft asked, his heart beginning to beat faster than the club's bass.

'Your brother,' Pete explained, still smiling. After a moment the grin slid from his face.

Because he knew he'd slipped.

Scowcroft knew it too, and trapped between the press of dancing bodies and the table, there was only one thing he could do.

So he slid the supermarket-bought kitchen knife from the sleeve of his shirt and prodded the tip into the man's belly.

'Who are you?' he hissed in the imposter's ear.

'You think you're the only one with a knife?' the man sneered. 'I've had mine pointed at your femoral artery since you sat down.' Scowcroft felt the press of a blade against the flesh of his thigh, his body shaking with the released adrenaline of his fight-or-flight survival instincts.

'Scared?' the man mocked, feeling the shaking muscles through the blade. 'Just hand over the diamonds.'

'Who sent you?' Scowcroft challenged, his eyes burning with fury, desperate now that the heist had fallen at the final hurdle.

'Marcus Slate,' the man growled, his own eyes equally alight with determination. 'Marcus Slate sent me, and I'm taking him back his diamonds.'

Scowcroft fought for control of his muscles, because the thought of flight had passed, and he knew there was only one thing left to do – fight.

So he did.

'Fuck you,' the thief spat as he drove the knife deep into the stomach of Slate's henchman.

'Fuck you,' he shouted again as he drove the knife into the stomach of Detective Inspector Hill.

# CHAPTER 33

HILL HAD NEVER BEEN stabbed before, and for a hundredth of a second he almost marvelled at the brilliant white pain that shot through his entire body.

And then, on instinct, he drove his own blade forward.

He felt it part flesh as it cut into the young man's thigh. He felt the spit on his face as his adversary howled in pain, the scream lost to the bass and revelry of the club. He felt the hot blood spurt over his hand as he pulled the blade free.

It was the blood on his hands that shook Hill from his instinctive reactions and brought him the realisation of what he had suffered, and what he'd done. Hill knew the gushing wound would kill the young man within minutes. There was no reclaiming the situation – he was committed now.

No, he realised. He'd been committed since the moment he'd told Slate he'd recover the man's diamonds, and avoid any trial that would cast a shadow over Slate's enterprise. He'd been committed to this end when he'd sold his soul to Slate for a million, the dream of his own business empire and a better life for himself and Deb.

Hill had never thought he'd have to kill for it.

The woman was pulling the young man away and half carrying him down the few steps that led out onto the dance floor, the dancing girls shooting angry stares as she barged by them.

Hill hesitated to follow – surely someone would see the blood? Surely someone would stop them?

But the club was dark, and the dying thief looked like one more drunken idiot. Seeing that they were already moving to the exit, where they would become someone else's problem, the bouncers did little more than roll their eyes and turn their attention back to the girls.

Hill saw his prize slipping away. And he knew what Slate would do to him if he didn't get those diamonds.

Everything had gone perfectly up until then. With the right kind of persuasion, Barrett had talked. Hill had then handed him over to Slate's men, to what end he didn't know, but he could guess. Then it had simply been a case of meeting the buyer, showing his police identification, and kindly telling the man to forget everything related to the sale of the stolen diamonds. 'Pete' had been more than happy to escape so lightly.

Now it had all gone to shit. Hill moved to stand, pulling his jacket closed across the wound. The knife had torn the muscles of his abdomen, each step causing pain to shoot through his body, but he would worry about the damage later. First he had to catch the thieves.

He had to catch them, and then he had to kill them.

## CHAPTER 34

'NOT THROUGH THE FRONT!' Scowcroft groaned through gritted teeth, seeing that Charlotte was leading them towards the club's main entrance. 'Security will stop us,' he managed, knowing that out on the street there would be no hiding the blood that flowed from his leg.

'We have to stop the bleeding!' Charlotte's eyes were wide as she pushed him into a dark recess amongst the club's shadows. 'Put your hands on it!' she shouted. 'Apply pressure!'

Scowcroft tried, but he was already weak from blood loss. He felt Charlotte free the belt from his trousers and pull it tight around the top of his thigh.

Then, as the blood slowed to a trickle, the agony built to unbearable. Scowcroft squeezed his eyes shut and cursed. 'I can't take it, Charlotte! Take it off!' he cried.

'No! You'll bleed to death!'

'Charlotte!' he pleaded. 'Take it off!'

Charlotte ignored the cries. Instead she punched Scowcroft in the stomach.

'Think about your brother, Alex,' she hissed at him. 'Man up!'

The savage tone of Charlotte's voice forced Scowcroft to try, clenching his jaw against the agony. She helped him up and over towards the club's toilets. Looking over her shoulder, Charlotte saw their assailant following through the crowded dance floor. The man moved slowly, not wanting to draw attention to himself, but his eyes were fixed on them.

The thieves staggered into the passageway that led to the toilets. Free from the crowd of the dance floor, individuals began to notice and go wide-eyed at the sight of the bloodied young man.

A suited gentleman stepped forwards and spoke to Charlotte in Dutch. She presumed he was offering to help, and did her best to show a carefree smile.

'Ambulance is coming out there, thank you,' she replied, using her free hand to point to the nearest fire escape.

'I will get it,' the man said in English, then trotted ahead to push open the door, cold air rushing into the corridor.

'Thank you,' Charlotte said, then slammed the door behind them. Letting go of Scowcroft, she quickly wheeled a heavy dustbin across the entrance to block the doorway, and then followed it with another.

'I've got to lie down,' Scowcroft said weakly and dropped heavily to the ground.

Charlotte heard banging against the fire escape, but the large bins held.

'You need a hospital. I'll get an ambulance.'

'No, they'll bring the police,' he groaned.

'A car then.'

'No. Just take them,' Scowcroft implored, pushing the diamonds into Charlotte's coat pocket. 'Take them. Find another buyer.'

'No,' Charlotte stated firmly, then threw her eyes up at the fire escape – the banging had stopped.

Scowcroft, weak as he was, also became aware of the silence. It was time to run.

'We can't both get away, Char, but you can,' he told her calmly. 'It's you and Tony making it, or you and me dead. Even I can do that maths. Come on. Get the fuck out of here.'

'I'm not leaving,' she promised, clutching the young man's hand. 'I'm not leaving,' she said again, as tears began to roll down her cheeks.

Because she knew he was dying.

Alex Scowcroft knew it too.

'I let him down,' he sobbed weakly, struggling to keep Charlotte's face in focus. 'I let Tony down, Charlotte. I couldn't finish this for him.'

'You've done everything a brother could do and more, Alex,' she told him, putting her hand against his greying face.

Scowcroft's eyelids shuddered as he tried to stay awake. He tried to fight, because he still had so many things he needed to say. Needed Charlotte to hear. That he was sorry. That she was, and always would be, the true guardian and soulmate of his brother.

But Alex Scowcroft could only gasp.

And then he slipped into the darkness.

# CHAPTER 35

**HILL PUSHED THE HEEL** of his hand against the knife wound in his abdomen. He knew the pressure would slow the bleeding and help the clots to form, but he hoped the pressure would also take away the pain he suffered with every step. Not wanting to draw attention in the club, he had taken his time in pursuit, but the blocked fire escape had meant he was forced to exit via the club's main entrance.

Luckily for him, Hill's dark suit hid most of the bloodstains, and with his hands pushed deep into his pockets, he was able to keep his face neutral as he walked by the bouncers. Clear of the club's front, Hill then tried to break into a run to its rear, but the pain in his stomach almost caused him to scream so he was forced to continue his chase at a walk. Despite the restriction, Hill at first took comfort in knowing that the thief would be in a worse condition, but then the cold realisation hit home that it was his own hand which had doomed the man, and he was racked by a wave of nausea born of guilt.

'Too late now,' he hissed, trying to convince himself.

The detective turned another corner, working his way between the stacks of empty beer kegs to the club's rear fire escape. With the young man's wound, they couldn't have got too far ahead – but then Hill saw that the young man hadn't got anywhere at all, and the long-time police officer knew from one look that the youngster was dead.

And so Hill was a murderer.

'Jesus Christ,' he groaned, then reminded himself he was a man with no time for remorse. Hill had made a pact with the devil, and if he didn't deliver on his end of the bargain, then he had no doubt his own skin would be as grey and waxen as that of the thief who lay before him.

'You got yourself into this, you stupid bastard,' he hissed at the corpse as he dropped to his knees and began to rummage through the boy's pockets. 'Sometimes shit things happen to the people you care about!' he went on, defending his actions. 'Life isn't a movie, you dumb piece of shit! There are consequences! Your actions have consequences!' Hill said to dead ears, before sitting back heavily.

Because he had found something in the pockets – a hard object, wrapped tightly in tape.

Hill used his knife to slit open the packaging, and then, dropping the blade to his side, he hastily unwrapped it with his bloodstained hands.

And he saw the diamond sparkling in the moonlight.

Hill swallowed, overcome by what the stone signified. Yes, it was beautiful, but it was also his future. The future he'd always wanted, for him and for Deb.

'Thank you.' He spoke aloud, though only Hill knew to whom the words were intended.

His final words.

Caught up in his own exoneration, Hill hadn't heard the fall of soft footsteps behind him. He hadn't heard the soft scrape on tarmac as his blade was plucked from the ground.

But he did feel it pierce his spine.

It was the last thing he'd experience in his life.

# EPILOGUE

## Two years later

Charlotte looked up from the pile of laundry placed in front of her, and ran her hands through her frayed hair. On days like this she hated the mundane routine that her life had become. Part of her – a part she hated – almost wished that Tony still needed her care and total dedication.

But Tony was his own man now, at least in body, she reminded herself sadly. In mind, he was consumed by grief and guilt. The thought of it was too much for Charlotte to bear, and as she did every day, she tried to lose herself in her mundane tasks, meticulously folding each item of laundry so that there wasn't a single wrinkle present.

An hour passed before there was a knock on the highly polished door.

'Hello?' a woman called from the threshold.

She had the city look about her, Charlotte noticed. Well spoken, and with a hairstyle that was yet to grow out. She was new, Charlotte decided.

'How long have you been inside?' she asked her fellow inmate.

'Here, only a week, but I've been moving around a bit.' The woman blushed. 'I'm supposed to help you.'

'So help.' Charlotte shrugged, two years in prison having blunted her manners.

And no wonder, because it had been a hard two years. For stabbing a police officer, Charlotte had suffered at the hands of every bobby and prison guard she'd come across since her arrest in Amsterdam.

'What can I do to help?' the fresh meat asked, but Charlotte was a world away now. She was back in the courtrooms, a sideshow of the media circus.

Charlotte wanted to puke when she thought of how Hill had become the darling of the tabloids – the hero who'd taken on a dangerous case in his final week of service. Scotland Yard were as happy as the media to take that line, glossing over coincidence. Only the keenest onlookers noted that Chief Inspector Vaughn, Hill's superior, had resigned his post at Scotland Yard and had been relocated to a small station in England's hinterland.

'You're the one that did in that detective, right?' the woman pushed, cutting into Charlotte's thoughts.

She wasn't surprised to hear the question. Amongst the criminal fraternity of prison, Charlotte enjoyed notoriety.

'Yeah,' she answered. 'That was me.'

Charlotte shrugged, going back to her task of folding sheets and thinking of how her vengeance had capped a story of crime and love that had gone viral across the world, attracting the attention of a generous benefactor who'd been moved to cover the costs of Tony's treatment.

'I read about it in the paper,' the woman said, struggling to fold her own pile of clothing. Charlotte noticed that her tiny hands were shaking. Funny, she thought, how people's attitudes had changed towards her.

'Leave the clothes,' Charlotte said, trying to sound pleasant. 'I'll just have to do them again anyway.'

'I'm sorry,' the woman said quickly.

'No. It's fine.'

'I'm just a bit nervous,' she explained. 'My husband, he's not well. He's quadriplegic, actually. I don't know how he's getting on without me.'

'I'm sorry to hear that,' Charlotte told her, her prison mask slipping. 'I know how that must feel.'

'I know. I read the stories. About you and your husband. That's why I asked them to put me with you, down here.'

'Oh. How long are you in for?'

'They gave me a couple of months, but I think it's going to be a lot longer than that,' the woman whispered.

'A couple of months?' Charlotte asked, confused – her prison catered to long-term inmates only.

'I knew some people – through my husband – guards, judges. They made it happen.'

'You wanted to come here?' Charlotte asked, taking a half-step back.

'Because I said I'd do something really bad.'

'What's your name?' Charlotte asked, suddenly uncomfortable. 'I'm Charlotte Scowcroft.' She tried to smile, putting out her hand.

'Deborah.' The woman grinned back, lifting her own hand from her pocket. 'But my husband called me Deb. Deb Hill.'

Too late, Charlotte saw the blade.

Evil has a new game...

Read on for an extract

**TWO MEN TROD CAREFULLY** through the trees in search of their prey. Bluebells and wild garlic were underfoot, beech and Douglas firs on all sides, tendrils of early morning fog still clinging to the damp slopes. Somewhere in this wood was the quarry.

The man in front, feeling brave, thanks to the morning sherry, his bolt-action Purdey and the security man covering his back, was Lord Oakleigh. A QC of impeccable education, with an impressive listing in *Debrett's* and his peer's robes tailored by Ede & Ravenscroft, Oakleigh had long ago decided that these accomplishments paled in comparison to the way he felt now – this particular mix of adrenalin and fear, this feeling of being so close to death.

*This*, he had decided, was life. And he was going to live it.

The car had collected him at 4 a.m. He'd taken the eye mask he was given, relaxed in the back of the Bentley and used the opportunity for sleep. In a couple of hours he arrived at the estate. He recognised some of his fellow hunters, but not all – there were a couple of Americans and a Japanese gentleman he'd never seen before. Nods were exchanged. Curtis and Boyd of The Quarry Co. made brief introductions. All weapons were checked to ensure they were smart-modified, then they were networked and synced to a central hub.

The tweed-wearing English contingent watched, bemused, as the Japanese gentleman's valet helped him into what looked like tailored disruptive-pattern clothing. Meanwhile the shoot security admired the TrackingPoint precision-guided rifle he carried. Like women fussing over a new baby, they all wanted a hold.

As hunt time approached, the players fell silent. Technicians wearing headphones unloaded observation drones from an operations van. Sherry on silver platters was brought round by blank-faced men in tails. Curtis and Boyd toasted the hunters and, in his absence, the quarry. Lastly, players were assigned their security – Oakleigh was given Alan, his regular man – before a distant report indicated that the hunt had begun and the players moved off along the lawns to the treeline, bristling with weaponry and quivering with expectation.

Now deep in the wood, Oakleigh heard the distant chug of Land Rover engines and quad bikes drift in on a light breeze. From overhead came the occasional buzz of a drone, but otherwise it was mostly silent, even more so the further into the wood they ventured and the more dense it became. It was just the way he liked it. Just him and his prey.

'Ahead, sir,' came Alan's voice, urgent enough that Oakleigh dropped to one knee and brought the Purdey to his shoulder in one slightly panicked movement. The wood loomed large in his cross hairs, the undergrowth keeping secrets.

'Nothing visible,' he called back over his shoulder, then cleared his throat and tried again, this time with less shaking in his voice. 'Nothing up ahead.'

'Just hold it there a moment or so, sir, if you would,' replied Alan, and Oakleigh heard him drop his assault rifle to its strap and reach for his walkie-talkie. 'This is red team. Request status report . . .'

'Anything, Alan?' Oakleigh asked over his shoulder.

'No, sir. No visuals from the drones. None of the players report any activity.'

'Then our boy is still hiding.'

'It would seem that way, sir.'

'Why is he not trying to make his way to the perimeter? That's what they usually do.'

'The first rule of combat is to do the opposite of what the enemy expects, sir.'

'But this isn't combat. This is a hunt.'

'Yes, sir.'

'And it isn't much of a hunt if the quarry's hiding, is it?' Oakleigh heard the note of indignation in his voice and knew it sounded less like genuine outrage and more like fear, so he put his eye back to the scope and swept the rifle barrel from left to right, trying to keep a lid on his nerves. He wanted a challenge. But he didn't want to die.

*Don't be stupid. You're not going to die.*

But then came the crackle of distant gunfire, quickly followed by a squall of static.

'Quarry spotted. Repeat: quarry spotted.'

Oakleigh's heart jackhammered and he found himself in two minds. On the one hand, he wanted to be in the thick of the action. Last night he'd even entertained thoughts of being the winning player, imagining the admiration of his fellow hunters, ripples that would extend outwards to London and the corridors of power, the private members' clubs of the Strand and chambers of the House.

On the other hand, now that the quarry had shown himself capable of evading the hunters and drones for so long, he felt differently.

From behind came a rustling sound and then a thump. Alan made a gurgling sound.

Oakleigh realised too late that something was wrong and wheeled around, fumbling with the rifle.

A shot rang out and Alan's walkie-talkie squawked.

'Red team, report. Repeat: red team, report.'

**COOKIE HAD BEEN HIDING** in the lower branches of a beech. From the tree he'd torn a decent-sized stick, not snapping it, but twisting so it came away with a jagged end. Not exactly sharp. But not blunt, either. It was better than nothing.

He'd watched the player and his bodyguard below, waiting for the right moment to strike.

Forget the nervous old guy. He had a beautiful Purdey, but he was shaking like a shitting dog. The bodyguard was dangerous, but the moment Cookie saw him drop his rifle to its strap, he knew the guy was dead meat.

Sure enough, the guard never knew what hit him. Neither of the hunters had bothered looking up, supreme predators that they were, and Cookie dropped silently behind Alan, bare feet on the cool woodland floor. As his left arm encircled Alan's neck, his elbow angled so that his target's carotid artery was fat, his right arm plunged the stick into the exposed flesh.

But the years of drugs and booze and sleeping rough had taken their toll, and even as he let Alan slide to the ground to bleed out in seconds, the old guy was spinning round and levelling his hunting rifle. And where once Cookie's reactions had been as fast as his brain, now the two were out of alignment.

Oakleigh pulled the trigger. Cookie had already seen that he was left-handed and knew how the weapon would pull, and so he twisted in the opposite direction. But even so, he was too slow.

He heard tree bark crack and saw splinters fly a microsecond after he heard the shot. A second later, pain flared along his side and he felt blood pool in the waistband of his jeans.

The stick was still in his hand, so he stepped forward and rammed it into the old guy's throat, cursing him for a coward, as Oakleigh folded to the ground with the stick protruding from his neck.

'Red team, report. Red team, report,' wailed the walkie-talkie. But even though Cookie knew others would be arriving soon, he needed a moment to compose himself, so he leaned against a tree, pressing his palm to the spot where the bullet had grazed him. He pulled up his sweater to inspect the wound. It looked bad, but he knew from painful experience it was nothing to worry about. Blood loss and the fact that he'd be easier to track were the worst of it.

He took stock. The old guy was still twitching. Alan was dead. Cookie reached for the security guard's assault rifle, but when he inspected the grip, he found it inset with some kind of sensor. His heart sank as he tried to operate the safety and found it unresponsive, knowing what the sensor meant: smart-technology. Linked to the user's palm print. And if his guess was correct . . .

*Fuck!* The old guy's Purdey was equipped with the same. He tossed it away. From Alan he took a hunting knife. The old guy had a sidearm, also smart-protected and also useless.

The hunting knife would have to do. But now it was time to find out if these Quarry Co. guys were going to fulfil their part of the bargain. He put a hand to his side and started running. Leaves stung his eyes. Twigs lashed him. He stumbled over roots bubbling on the ground and reached to push branches aside as he hurtled forward in search of sanctuary.

From behind came the crash of gunfire. Overhead the sound of the drones intensified. They'd spotted him now. The time for stealth was over. He just had to hope he'd given them enough to think about in the meantime, and that the two casualties would slow them down.

Teeth bared, hatred in his bones, he kept running. The trees were thinning. Ahead of him was a peat-covered slope and he hit it fast. Scrambling to the top, he was painfully aware that he'd made himself a visible target, but he was close now. Close to the perimeter.

'If you reach the road you win. The money's yours.'

'No matter who I have to kill along the way?'

'Our players expect danger, Mr Cook. What is the roulette wheel without the risk of losing?'

He'd believed them and, fuck it, why not?

And there it was – the road. It bisected a further stretch of woodland, but this was definitely it. An observation drone buzzed a few feet above him. To his left he heard the sound of approaching engines and saw a Land Rover Defender leaning into the bend, approaching fast. Two men in the front.

They didn't look like they were about to celebrate his victory. He tensed. At his rear the noise of the approaching hunting party was getting louder.

The Defender roared up to his position, passenger door flapping as it drew to a halt. A security guy wielding the same Heckler & Koch assault rifle carried by Alan stepped out and took up position behind the door.

'Where's my money?' called Cookie, with a glance back down into the basin of the wood. He could see the blurry outlines of players and their security among the trees, the crackle of comms. 'You said if I reached the road I win,' he pressed.

Ignoring him, the passenger had braced his rifle on the sill of his window and was speaking into a walkie-talkie, saying something Cookie couldn't hear. Receiving orders.

'Come on, you bastards. I reached the fucking road, now where's my money?'

The passenger had finished on the walkie-talkie, and Cookie had been shot at enough times to know the signs of it happening again. There was no prize money. No winning. No survival. There were just hunters and prey. Just an old fool and a man about to gun him down.

The passenger squeezed off bullets that zinged over Cookie's head as he tucked in and let himself roll back to the bottom of the slope.

*I can do this*, he thought. He'd fought in Afghanistan. He'd fought with the best, against the best. He could go up against a bunch of rich geriatric thrill-seekers and come out on top – security or no security. *Yes*. He was going to get out of this and then he was going to make the fuckers pay.

He could do it. Who dares wins.

Then a bullet ripped the top of Cookie's head off – a bullet fired from a TrackingPoint precision-guided bolt-action rifle.

'Oh, good shot, Mr Miyake,' said the players as they emerged from the undergrowth in order to survey the kill.

They were already looking forward to the post-hunt meal.

**IT WAS DARK AND** Shelley was ground down after fruitless hours in various London shitholes, when trouble leaned on the bar.

It was the last place he'd intended to visit that day: the Two Dogs on Exmouth Market, a pub that was always open and always gloomy inside, forbidding to all but the early morning traders, afternoon postal workers from nearby Mount Pleasant and gangs of rail-link labourers who descended at night-time.

Shelley had cast an eye across the gathered throng with a sinking heart, sensing he'd get no joy from this lot. Most were already half in the bag. They were likely to give him the runaround, just for the hell of it.

So, a wasted day. The only thing to say for it was that Lucy would be proud. They'd both known there was a danger he'd simply dig in at the first pub he visited, emerging a day later with a hangover and a bad case of drinker's guilt. But no. All temptation and even the odd invitation had been resisted. He'd done the rounds as sober as a judge. A man on a mission.

Word of which had evidently got round, if the guy leaning on the bar was anything to go by.

'You're looking for somebody, I hear?' he said now, with a voice like a cement mixer.

Shelley stared into rheumy, drink-sodden eyes and knew a shakedown when he saw one. After all, with his black woollen overcoat and baker-boy cap tilted rakishly, he knew he stood out. That was the plan. But the same presence that made him a serious customer also made him a target for shakedowns and, from the looks of things, matey-boy here had in mind something more ambitious than a drink in return for yet more useless information. There was the knife he was wearing, for one thing.

'Yeah, I'm looking for someone,' smiled Shelley.

'Your brother, is it?' rasped the drunk. He wore an Adidas tracksuit top zipped to the neck. He had an air of menace that was as distinctive and recognisable to Shelley as the smell of shit.

'No, he's not my brother. A friend.'

*Best friend*, he thought. *Always got your back.*

'Brothers in arms, though, isn't it? You were in the forces together – you and this mate you're looking for.'

That was interesting. The guy was unfazed by Shelley's background. Which meant either he was very stupid or he had backup somewhere.

Shelley leaned towards him. 'You're right, mate. Yeah, we served in the SAS together. Cookie and I were part of a covert three-man team operating in Afghanistan. We carried out assassinations, broke up kidnapping attempts, interrogated suspects. All three of us in the team were highly trained in surveillance, counterintelligence, situational awareness and marksmanship. Each of us was expert in unarmed combat – a combination of Filipino Kali, Krav Maga and Jeet Kune Do, with a bit of street-fighting thrown in for good measure, just because we liked it that way. We were anti-fragile. You know what that means? It means the worse shit gets, the more efficient you are.

'See, that knife you're carrying in the waistband of your jeans, Cookie would take a pre-emptive approach it. And knowing him as I do, which is very well indeed, he'd use one of those pint glasses as a field-expedient weapon. He'd glass you, take the knife and you'd be picking bits of pint pot out of your throat while he was taking the piss out of you, for not keeping your blade sharp enough.

'Thing is, Cookie was always a touch more reckless than me. Hit them first, hit them hard and make sure they know they'd been hit, that was his motto. Me, I'm a bit more "by the book". I'd wait for you to draw the knife before I took it off you, and I'd break your arm doing it, *then* I'd take the piss out of you for not keeping it sharp enough.

'And so, knowing all that. Knowing now what you're dealing with here, how about you tell me any information you have? If it's useful, I can assure you I'll be grateful. Otherwise, you better take your knife and make yourself scarce before I get the wrong idea and decide to do things the Cookie way.'

The drunk affected a hurt look. 'Well, if you're going to be like that, you can shove it where the sun don't shine,' he spat, then pushed himself off the bar and out of Shelley's orbit.

Shelley sighed and turned his attention to the barman, producing the same snapshot of Cookie that he'd shown at least a dozen barmen that day. The guy barely gave it a look, before shrugging and moving away.

*That shrug, it must be in the manual*, thought Shelley. His eyes went to the mirror behind the bar and he watched the drunk skulk out of the door, thinking that he hadn't seen the last of that one.

He was right about that.

# JAMES PATTERSON
# BOOK**SHOTS**
## OUT THIS MONTH

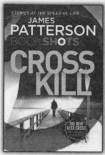

*Along Came a Spider* killer Gary Soneji died years ago. But Alex Cross swears he sees Soneji gun down his partner. Is his greatest enemy back from the grave?

Humans are evolving into a savage new species that could save civilisation – or end it. *Zoo* was just the beginning.

Detective Harry Blue is determined to take down the serial killer who's abducted several women, but her mission leads to a shocking revelation.

A royal is kidnapped the day before the Trooping the Colour parade. Can Private's Jack Morgan save the day before kidnap turns to murder?

A world-famous tennis player is stalked from Roland Garros to Wimbledon by a deadly killer intent on destroying more than just her career.

Two rival crews attempt to steal millions of pounds' worth of diamonds at exactly the same time, leading to a thrilling high-speed chase across Europe.

When former SAS captain David Shelley goes looking for a missing friend, he enters into the same danger that may have got his friend killed.

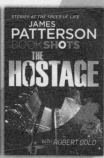

A man is thrown from the top floor of a glamorous new London hotel. Can Head of Security John Roscoe find the killer before the bodies pile up?

# JAMES PATTERSON
# BOOKSHOTS
## COMING SOON

### AIRPORT: CODE RED

A major terrorist cell sets a devastating plan in motion.
Their target? One of the world's busiest airports.

### THE TRIAL: A WOMEN'S MURDER CLUB THRILLER

An accused killer will do anything to disrupt his own trial, including
a courtroom shocker that Lindsay Boxer will never see coming.

### LITTLE BLACK DRESS

Can a little black dress change everything? What begins
as one woman's fantasy is about to go too far.

### LEARNING TO RIDE

City girl Madeline Harper never wanted to love a cowboy. But rodeo
king Tanner Callen might change her mind... and win her heart.

# ALSO BY JAMES PATTERSON

### ALEX CROSS NOVELS

Along Came a Spider
Kiss the Girls
Jack and Jill
Cat and Mouse
Pop Goes the Weasel
Roses are Red
Violets are Blue
Four Blind Mice
The Big Bad Wolf
London Bridges
Mary, Mary
Cross
Double Cross
Cross Country
Alex Cross's Trial (*with Richard DiLallo*)
I, Alex Cross
Cross Fire
Kill Alex Cross
Merry Christmas, Alex Cross
Alex Cross, Run
Cross My Heart
Hope to Die
Cross Justice

### THE WOMEN'S MURDER CLUB SERIES

1st to Die
2nd Chance (*with Andrew Gross*)
3rd Degree (*with Andrew Gross*)

4th of July (*with Maxine Paetro*)
The 5th Horseman (*with Maxine Paetro*)
The 6th Target (*with Maxine Paetro*)
7th Heaven (*with Maxine Paetro*)
8th Confession (*with Maxine Paetro*)
9th Judgement (*with Maxine Paetro*)
10th Anniversary (*with Maxine Paetro*)
11th Hour (*with Maxine Paetro*)
12th of Never (*with Maxine Paetro*)
Unlucky 13 (*with Maxine Paetro*)
14th Deadly Sin (*with Maxine Paetro*)
15th Affair (*with Maxine Paetro*)

### DETECTIVE MICHAEL BENNETT SERIES

Step on a Crack (*with Michael Ledwidge*)
Run for Your Life (*with Michael Ledwidge*)
Worst Case (*with Michael Ledwidge*)
Tick Tock (*with Michael Ledwidge*)
I, Michael Bennett (*with Michael Ledwidge*)
Gone (*with Michael Ledwidge*)
Burn (*with Michael Ledwidge*)
Alert (*with Michael Ledwidge*)

### PRIVATE NOVELS

Private (*with Maxine Paetro*)
Private London (*with Mark Pearson*)

Private Games (*with Mark Sullivan*)

Private: No. 1 Suspect (*with Maxine Paetro*)

Private Berlin (*with Mark Sullivan*)

Private Down Under (*with Michael White*)

Private L.A. (*with Mark Sullivan*)

Private India (*with Ashwin Sanghi*)

Private Vegas (*with Maxine Paetro*)

Private Sydney (*with Kathryn Fox*)

Private Paris (*with Mark Sullivan*)

## NYPD RED SERIES

NYPD Red (*with Marshall Karp*)

NYPD Red 2 (*with Marshall Karp*)

NYPD Red 3 (*with Marshall Karp*)

NYPD Red 4 (*with Marshall Karp*)

## STAND-ALONE THRILLERS

Sail (*with Howard Roughan*)

Swimsuit (*with Maxine Paetro*)

Don't Blink (*with Howard Roughan*)

Postcard Killers (*with Liza Marklund*)

Toys (*with Neil McMahon*)

Now You See Her (*with Michael Ledwidge*)

Kill Me If You Can (*with Marshall Karp*)

Guilty Wives (*with David Ellis*)

Zoo (*with Michael Ledwidge*)

Second Honeymoon (*with Howard Roughan*)

Mistress (*with David Ellis*)

Invisible (*with David Ellis*)

The Thomas Berryman Number

Truth or Die (*with Howard Roughan*)

Murder House (*with David Ellis*)

## NON-FICTION

Torn Apart (*with Hal and Cory Friedman*)

The Murder of King Tut (*with Martin Dugard*)

## ROMANCE

Sundays at Tiffany's (*with Gabrielle Charbonnet*)

The Christmas Wedding (*with Richard DiLallo*)

First Love (*with Emily Raymond*)

## OTHER TITLES

Miracle at Augusta (*with Peter de Jonge*)